I0631823

WRATH

JoJo
PUBLISHING

Wrath
Anne Davies

Published by Classic Author and Publishing Services Pty Ltd
An imprint of Jo Jo Publishing.
First published 2014

'Yarra's Edge'
2203/80 Lorimer Street
Docklands VIC 3008
Australia

Email: jo-media@bigpond.net.au or visit www.classic-jojo.com

© Anne Davies

JoJo Publishing

Designer / typesetter: Chameleon Print Design

Editor: Julie Athanasiou

Printed in Singapore by KHL Printing

National Library of Australia Cataloguing-in-Publication entry

Author:	Davies, Anne, author.
Title:	Wrath : after committing an horrific crime can Luca finally achieve redemption / Anne Davies.
ISBN:	9780987607737 (paperback)
Target Audience:	For secondary school age.
Subjects:	Murder--Tennessee--Juvenile fiction.
	Criminals--Tennessee--Biography--Juvenile fiction.
Dewey Number:	A823.4

WRATH

ANNE DAVIES

PROLOGUE

I've never been in a courtroom before. There's something creepy about it. I don't know if it's all that old wood everywhere with panelling on the walls, doors, benches, and rails—a bit like a coffin, really. It's how I imagine it might be after you die, sitting and waiting to see if you're going to be sent to Heaven or Hell. Not that I believe in any of that crap. When you're dead, you're dead. Kaputzki! That's all, folks.

Look at that old codger behind the bench up there. He's the one who's going to finally say what happens to me. What makes him God? He will decide whether I'm guilty or not. That shouldn't be too hard. I rang the cops and said I'd killed him—them. Hardly rocket science.

The panel comes in and sits down. I don't get a real jury because of my age. I look at them one by one with my toughest face on, the one where I make my eyes go kind of dead.

1

First there's a man of about 50, I guess, and he doesn't really want to be here. I can tell. He's sneaking a look at the clock on the wall behind the judge's head. His shirt and tie look cheap and tacky, like he's dressed for a funeral. Maybe he is.

My heart thumps, and I make it calm down. Don't think. Just look. I can't really see the rest of him from where I'm sitting. He sees me looking at him and looks away fast.

There's a woman next to him. She looks like someone's kind grandmother, with hair like white fairy floss in a bun on top of her head and a powdery, lined face. She catches me looking at her too and swivels her head down quickly.

One by one, I scan them, feeling like a robot or maybe one of those clown things at the Royal Show— the ones that turn their heads while you drop balls down their gaping mouths. I wish I were a machine too—no feelings—but as I think that, it happens: that horrible, deep, dark…what can I call it? Tingle? No, that's not strong enough. It's like a deep electrical shock running through my body—up my legs, down my arms. It's bad, really bad. I feel like I'm going to fall.

I'm not a machine! I want to shout. *I'm a boy! I'm real, and I want to go home now! Make all this stop!* But

I have no home—no mother, no father, no sister…and no stepfather either. Can he really be gone forever? Thank God! Not that God wants to be thanked by me. Not after what I did. When I die, I'll go to Hell… Oh, bullshit. Don't fall for all that bullshit. But what if…? Just shut up! Shut up!

I hear a voice. It's Mr Bloom. "Are you all right, Luca? You're twitching and mumbling. Keep calm!" he whispers. I nod and concentrate on breathing slower than slow so that everything fades and there's nothing but the drone of voices…

CHAPTER ONE

Last night, I dreamed I was flying. I know heaps of kids who say they've dreamed that. Why is that? Maybe because we're kind of chained to the earth. Think about it. Nearly every sport there is tries to free us from the dirt, if only for a moment. We try to jump higher, longer; we run so we can leap away; we swim so we can know weightlessness; we climb mountains, ice skate, paraglide. So if we're supposed to have 'come from dust', why are we so desperate to get away from it?

Anyway, my dream: I was flying. I can't exactly remember how I got in the air, but I felt so good. The wind was warm in my face, and there was no sound except for the wind's hiss in my ears as I swooped and glided. I looked down, and the earth below me—which had been so neatly drawn up into rectangles of emerald, lime and yellow—began changing, and I felt panic. I could see beneath the green, and it was not controlled by lines but by mouldy seething brown. I was falling towards it faster and faster.

The wind was screaming in my ears now—or was that my screaming?—and I knew that if I hit the ground, I would be dead, but I *did* hit it and just passed straight through. Now there was no wind in my ears—only silence and darkness—but I kept on falling, and I knew it would never stop. Then I woke with a jump, shouting garbled, strangled sounds.

I lay in the dark, panting and almost glad to have woken up in my bed, even if this cell is a type of grave, a type of earthless burrow where I'll be stuck forever. I know I'm trapped here. I'm in here for 23 out of 24 hours at the moment, 'under observation'. That may change, or maybe I'll have no one to talk to—ever. No way I'm going to talk to that psych the court appointed. But there is somebody… There's you. I can talk to you. I know you'll never answer, but you're out there. I'll write everything down—not like those 'Dear Diary' things that girls write in and giggle over, all little plastic locks and pink butterflies—no, I'm writing to you. I know you're out there; I can feel you there.

I want to go over all of this in my mind to get it straight—no, not in my mind; I get all messed up and panicky when I think all the time. I want to write it down. It *has* to be orderly then—not one thought crowding another out. I just want to tell you everything that's happened so you can help me make sense of it, help me understand. I need to know there's someone out there who's listening to me. I know it's not possible, but unless I do this, I'm going to go nuts. I can feel insanity creeping up on me. I won't even imagine you as a woman or a man, old or young—just someone who'll hear me out and help me.

Just listen to me. Please.

I'll start right at the beginning. We were born near Geraldton, a town on the coast of Western Australia, if you haven't heard of it. I'll just explain that 'we' first. I'm a twin, so I've never really felt that saying 'I was born' sounds right. I was born first and then 10 minutes later, Katy. It's a funny thought that we were squashed up together, floating around and maybe battling for room near the end, sleeping and growing in that reddish glow that must be the womb. How many old grans have made that joke! "Oh, you're a pair of womb mates!" And they cackle away as though they've just made the most hilarious joke in history.

I wonder how it was decided that I came first? I was a bit bigger than Katy, so I probably muscled my way down, head locked in position like a torpedo, and then boom! Out we came like two slippery fish, my mother said. Mum, you gave me life and then I took yours away. God help me. But I'm not going to think about that now. I'm not going to think about what's happening now at all. I'm just going back. Trying to remember my life, my existence when I did exist, out there.

Home was a typical little country town half an hour's drive from Geraldton. There was really just a pub, a shop that sold everything from farm machinery to flour to razor blades, a post office, a Catholic church, a hall, a railway station and a cluster of little houses with red tin roofs and saggy fences. The school was a 20-minute walk away from my house, sandwiched between the Anglican church and the river. Just up the road from home was the football oval with a couple of corrugated iron lean-tos—one for our supporters and one for the opposing team's—and a dry, dusty tennis court with sprigs of grass groping up through the cracks.

My first memories are of our room. Katy and I didn't exactly share a room; it was a sleep-out that Dad had made by filling in the L-shaped veranda that went around the front and side of our little house. Katy's bed was at one end of the L and mine was at the other, so we couldn't see each other around the corner, but we could hear each other and talk as much as we liked.

We thought it was perfect. Katy would say, "It's good that we've got our own space but we're still kind of together. That's how it'll always be, won't it, Luca? Wherever you are, even if I can't see you, I know you'll be just around the corner and you'll be able to hear me one way or another."

And I'd say, "Always, Katy. We'll always be near each other. And when we die, we'll die at the same time, just like how we were born at the same time."

Funny; I always thought I had hardly any memory at all of when I was a little kid, but somehow being in here and being so quiet has made things jump out at me from the past. It's like the past is murky water and now that everything's still, all the dirt's settled on the bottom and bits are starting to clear. Or maybe it's just because I'm writing it down so I can tell you about it. Who knows? Anyway, I like it. It reminds me that I'm more than just a lump of meat locked in a cell.

Katy and I both got Dad's black hair, but mine's fairly curly while Katy's is just soft and wavy. Come to think of it, it's like she got the softer version all the way. Her eyes are big and blue; mine are dark. Her nose is a smaller version of mine—lucky for her, because mine is huge. Her mouth is small and full; mine is a line with hardly any lips at all. Despite all that, you can still tell we're twins, easy!

Her name's cute and soft too—whereas mine...! What were they thinking? Mum says there was a song she used to like which had the first line 'My name is Luca' and then when she met Dad, he told her he'd gotten his black curly hair from his grandfather, whose name was Luca, in Italy. That clinched it for her. She thought it was a sign. Kids at school called me 'Lucy'. Great.

Dad was a mechanic, and he had a big workshop out the back. The back yard wasn't too pretty, with cars and trucks waiting to be repaired and car parts spilling out of the shed, but I loved it. Just walking outside and into that shed made me want to hurry and grow up. It smelt like man stuff, and Dad smelt that way too. Kind of an oily, tangy, slightly sweaty smell with a mix of a whole lot of stuff I can't really name. Dad went out to the farms to fix the tractors, trucks, generators and pumps. He did okay even though most people on the land are pretty handy.

Mum was always trying to get some flowers to grow out there, but with all the customers' boots and greasy water sluicing out over the ground, she had no hope.

She'd say, "Just a few roses for the house; just a spot for some vegetables," and she'd work away, trying to keep the sun from shrivelling those little plants to death if they'd made it past everything else. But they'd all die, no matter what. It seemed to be such a big thing to her.

I'd said to her once, when she was down on her knees pulling out all those dried up little plant bodies, "Don't worry about it, Mum. Just buy some veggies and flowers," but she'd turned on me, her eyes filling with tears, and she'd said, "You just don't understand! I've got to get something to grow."

Then in a day or two, there she'd be with a new packet of seeds, down on her knees in that gravelly red dirt, planting each one and tucking it in like it was a newborn baby. Her face would be all smiley and soft, and she'd look up at me and say, "Maybe this time, Luca. I feel like these ones are going to grow." 'Course they never did.

I found out a lot later why she was so upset. One night, when I got up to go out the back, I heard her snuffling away and Dad murmuring soft, and then her voice rose and she said, "But Dan, even the cow in the paddock can drop a calf. I've done it before. Why can't I do it again?" I couldn't hear what Dad said, but I went back to bed a bit stunned. I'd never thought Mum would want more than just Katy and me. Any other kid would be the odd one out here. I shook my head and rolled over. A pity those plants wouldn't grow, maybe then she'd forget about growing more kids.

Apart from that, life rolled on, one day pretty much the same as the next. Katy and I would play together, with her making up stories and mud pies, and me building cities, roads, bridges and wharves out of all the nuts and bolts, bricks and odd tins that littered our yard, near each other but rarely doing the same thing.

Sometimes, Dad would shout, "Luca! Come and give me a hand," and I'd drop what I had in my hand and run to the shed. I really didn't do much, just clean up or sort screws into their different containers, but what I loved was the talk. Dad would start, and I'd just open my ears and brain and suck it in. He'd always talk about his family. I can see it now, the light slanting in through the clear panels he'd put in the roof, dust dancing in the rays. He'd lean back on the bench and file away at some rusty old bit of metal till it was just the shape and size he wanted. I'd see the dust streaked in the sweat down his forehead, his olive skin gleaming.

"Have I ever told you about my brother Peter?" he'd say, and though I knew it all by heart, I'd shake my head. "No, Dad, not really."

"He was the eldest in our family. First Peter, then Anthony, then Philippa, then me. He was eight years older than me, but he was the one I loved the most. He used to take me with him whenever he went out with his mates. They would get a bit sick of me tagging along, I think. We'd go down to the river and swim, and if any of the boys got too rough with me, Peter would grab them and threaten to flatten them. His eyes would flash, and he'd grit his teeth as he spoke, and even I got frightened.

"One day, one of the boys, Jeremy Muir, said, 'But Peter, why don't you leave him home sometimes? He's just a little pest.'

"'He's my brother,' Peter said flatly.

"'I know, but we're your friends.'

"Peter smiled at him. 'I know that, but you may not always be my friends. He will always be my brother. He wants to come, and I want him here. If you don't like it, swim somewhere else.'

"That's how he was, Luca. Family first—always. You remember that." And I'd nod and sort some screws, and we'd both be silent. I loved those times.

Got to stop now. Meal time. The siren's just gone, so in a minute the door will swing open, and there will be the guard. I can hear doors opening and the sound of footsteps getting louder as he gets closer.

13

CHAPTER TWO

The door rasps open, and I look up, expecting the guard to put a tray of food on the small desk in the corner. Instead, he says, "Right, sport. No more room service. Time to join everyone else in the dining room."

I look up at him, taking in the grey, clipped hair, the blue eyes, the blank expression and the name tag on his shirt that says 'Owen'.

"Come on, look lively!"

I jump off the bed and move towards the door.

"Wait till I'm outside!" he barks, turning and leaving my room. I walk to the door and step outside. To my left, I see a row of boys, mostly a bit older than me, I think, stretching back to the end of a wide corridor. Across the gap to the other side, there is another row of boys in a line, shuffling towards a pair of large swing doors at the end of the building.

The boys are all dressed like me, in navy-blue track pants and T-shirts.

One of them is staring at me, his face hard. His orange hair clashes oddly with his red face, and he glowers at me as though he hates me. Then I realise that he is at the head of the row and they are all waiting for me to get in line and start walking. I turn to the right and step in behind the guard. He strides off towards the doors, which open with a loud whirring noise as we get closer.

Beyond the doors is a large room so brightly lit that I wince, with rows of tables and benches. On the back wall is a line of older boys standing behind steaming pots of food, large ladles ready in their hands. The boys in the long line I had seen on the other side of the corridor are grabbing trays, and as they file past each upraised ladle, food is tipped onto their plates. As the line moves along, there is no talk, just the sound of the plates rattling and shoes scuffing across the grey linoleum floor.

I follow the guard to the end of the first line, and then he steps back, motioning me forward with an impatient wave. I take a tray from the pile and step back to the line to wait my turn for the food. He nudges me and mutters, "Table Five."

15

I turn and see numbers in metal holders in the middle of each table, and then it is my turn at the first counter.

"Soup?"

I nod, and a quick ladleful is dropped in a bowl and pushed towards me. I put it on my tray and then move along. The food looks watery, but there is plenty of it—boiled potatoes, beans, carrots, sausages—and I nod for all of it. At the end of the counter are tubs of yoghurt and small dishes of jelly and custard. I load up, shoving the plates close together to make room, and then, eyes straight ahead, I walk to Table Five.

Boys sit on the benches lining the tables all over the room, and low chatter and the odd laugh merges into a low, swelling undercurrent of noise. I put my tray on the table, step over the bench and sit down, trying not to hunch over too much, and then I start eating the soup slowly even though I want to slurp it down fast, grab the tray and run back to my room.

"What ya' in for, Skinny?"

I force myself to count to five and then turn and look straight at the rat-faced boy next to me.

"Flattening arseholes with big mouths," I say quietly and then keep eating my soup. I will my hand to keep steady, but my heart is jumping.

A laugh bursts out of the dark boy opposite me. "Good answer, kid," he says.

I look up, keeping my face blank. He's about 17, with a snub nose and warm, deep-set eyes, his round face split with the white grin of his teeth. The only thing really memorable about him is his build. I could only see him waist up, but man, is he a tank! The T-shirt he wears isn't baggy like mine or that of any of the others at the table, for that matter, but stretches taut across his swelling chest, the bands of the arms and neck straining around the bulge of his muscles.

"What's your name?" he asks.

"Luca."

He nods, not making any comment, and then smiles. "Luca, the smart-arse next to you is Tim, next to him is Johnno, then Aaron—he's the brains around here—and there's me, Archie. I'm the brawn."

I look in turn at each face. Tim squints back at me with that shy, eager look of a weak kid whose only hope is to attach himself to someone stronger by ingratiating himself. That's what he was trying to do with his comment to me—ingratiate himself to Archie, who looked to be the boss man of this little group, by making him laugh. Johnno sits next to him. He gives me an unsmiling, appraising stare, nods almost imperceptibly, and then turns back to his food. Aaron sits opposite him, next to Archie. He looks at me coolly through clear blue eyes. He has the face of an angel—short blond hair, firm mouth, strong jaw and nose—but it's those eyes, deep and searching, that hold my gaze.

He smiles, says, "Hi, Luca," and holds out his hand across the table. I take it without hesitation and nod. What the hell could he have done? Whatever it was certainly didn't show on his face. I knew though, instinctively, that asking that question would be a mistake, just as it had been when Tim asked it. Nobody's business.

Archie is leaning back in his chair, a smile on his face, and he looks at me expectantly. "Anything you want to know about the place?"

I hesitate and glance around the room, which is now noisy as the boys use their mouths as much for talking as they had been for eating. "I guess you're the main man around here," I say.

He raises an eyebrow. "You applying for the job?"

I shake my head. "Nuh. Just figured you were by the way you're built."

"Size doesn't make a guy the boss," says Aaron, shrugging. "No real bosses amongst the guys here. Just people who are okay and people who are dangerous bastards."

"Well, who's the most dangerous here, then?" I ask.

"Don't turn around real obvious, but three tables across, there's a big guy with tats on his face they call 'King'—not 'cause he's a boss but because his real name is Neil Brown."

I look blankly around the table, and they laugh.

"Never heard of a King Brown?"

"What, the snake?" I answer, puzzled.

"Yeah, the snake," says Aaron quietly, glancing across at the other table. The others look at him, forks suspended above their plates. "Did you know it's got more venom than any other snake?"

I shrug. "I know that if you get bitten by one, you're pretty much dead."

"Well, unless you happen to get bitten by one right outside the hospital, you're pretty much right. The thing with them, though, is they just won't get you once; they'll keep striking you over and over, more venom pumping in each time." Aaron pauses, spears a piece of sausage with his fork and then chews on it slowly. "That's why we call him 'King Brown'. You cross that mongrel, and he won't let up. He'll make it his sole mission in life to make your life hell. His brain isn't big, but man, once it latches onto something, he doesn't let go."

The table is silent apart from the sounds of the boys' eating. I am interested, despite myself. I had come in here determined to sit down, eat up and shut up, but I want to know a bit more. I open my mouth to speak, but the siren blasts and everyone shovels and slurps the last bit of food down. A guard moves to each table in turn, and the boys stand and take their plates and cups to a long bench at the back of the room, where they scrape the crumbs from each plate into a bin, place the plate in a stack, and then line up at the double doors where the guards are waiting. It's all so smooth.

I flick my eyes across to that King Brown kid and notice that even he goes through the motions quickly. He might be called King Brown, but he's still just a trapped worm in here like me.

CHAPTER THREE

We file back to our cells. I notice that the boys pretty much all go into their cells in pairs except me and a few others. That Brown kid goes in alone, I see. The guard closes my door, and I lie down. I start thinking about the kids I talked to. Had any of them done anything as bad as what I did? I don't really want to know, do I? I just don't want to get connected to people again—just you. I know you'll always be there. But my mind is jumping around. I'm not in the mood to write. I just want to go over everything that happened. Does it mean all my meals will be out there now? Can't write now, mind too jumpy.

*

I've calmed down a bit now. Guess it was just being amongst people after being alone for so long. Better that I'm on my own.

I guess when I was about seven or eight, things changed. Not so many cars came to our place anymore, and Dad didn't get many calls for work. He got quieter and quieter and stayed out in his shed longer but didn't seem to want to talk when I hung around. He and Mum didn't seem to talk together anymore either.

One night, we were sitting silently at the table eating soup. Mum sat at one end of the table, Dad sat at the other, and Katy and I sat in-between them. There were no jokes, no talking—just the slow ticking of the clock on the wall and the sounds of us eating. Each time I swallowed, I made a strange gulping sound. My throat seemed to be closing instead of opening to take in my food, and the sound seemed so loud in the quiet room.

"Eat properly, Luca!" Dad said, his thick eyebrows lowering.

"Leave him alone! He's just trying to eat. Don't take your bad mood out on him!" Mum's voice was shaking—with what, I didn't know. Anger? Fear? It wasn't worth all this. Dad hadn't really growled at me.

Turning slowly towards Mum, Dad put his spoon down deliberately. "My bad mood, is it? What am I supposed to be like when all my business has gone down the tubes? Should I maybe do a little dance for you? Should I laugh and sing about how all the people I know here, people I grew up with and thought were my friends, have stopped bringing their cars to me to fix because they can save $20 by going to Cants?"

Dad's voice had been getting louder and faster as he spoke, and as he spat out the word 'Cants', he slapped his hand down onto the table. The plates all jumped and clinked, and Katy's soup bowl tipped and hot soup slopped out onto the table, bits of carrots and celery clumping in a mound on the check cloth.

"Christ!" Dad shouted, turning and striding out of the room, his chair tipping onto its side and landing on the floor with a thud. We heard the back door bang shut and then there was silence again—just the tick tock of the clock. I was too afraid to look over at Mum, but Katy was sniffing a bit and I glanced across at her. Tears were glistening in her eyes, and she brushed them away quickly, her forehead crinkling in anger—at herself, I knew.

"Clear the table and then go straight to bed," my mother said in a hard voice.

Katy and I leapt up together and stacked the plates and cutlery in the sink, and then we both went up to Mum, who sat holding her head in her hands. I thought she was crying, but when we mumbled, "Good night, Mum," she raised her head, and her eyes were dry and cold, her mouth set in a narrow line.

"Okay, off you go," she said, and sensing there'd be no kiss or bedtime story tonight, we both turned and went to our room. I climbed into bed silently. Usually, Katy and I would chatter away to each other about school, but not tonight. I lay there feeling agitated but not really wanting to think about it. We both switched off our bedside lights at the same time, and then there was silence. Katy's bed creaked, I heard her bare feet whispering over the boards, and I opened the blankets for her to slide in beside me. She snuggled into my back without a word, and then we were asleep.

Dad didn't come home the next night, but the next day when we got home from school, we saw his car. Wordlessly, we dropped our bags and ran inside. He was sitting with Mum. Katy ran up to him and hugged him, and he swung her onto his lap then pulled a chair close to him for me. I sat down, and Mum jumped up to get us something to eat.

"Well, kids, there's something I've got to tell you. I've got a job driving a truck. I'll be driving all over the place from right up north and east as far as Kalgoorlie all through the wheat belt down to Perth." He stopped, and my mind raced.

"But when will you be home?" I rasped, my throat dry. He glanced at my mother, and she turned away, her mouth in that thin, hard line again.

"I won't be home that much, Luca. Maybe every couple of weeks."

Katy started to cry. "But I want you home all the time!" she sobbed. "Why can't you just fix everybody's cars and stay home?"

"Because no one wants me to do that anymore, Katy. There's a new big place opened up in Dongara, and it's got lots of fancy things for checking people's cars. It's got computers and lots of cheap parts, and they even sell petrol." His face hardened. "All I can do is fix cars." He was silent for a minute, and then his face brightened and he said, "It'll be fine. I'll be able to bring you things from Perth, and we'll have great fun when I'm home."

"I don't want anything from Perth. I just want you," I said, my voice quivering in a way I hated. I sounded like a baby.

"Well, Luca, that's the way it's going to have to be from now on. You'll be the man of the house while I'm not here, so I want you to help Mum as much as you can and look after your sister. And Katy, you're the same age as Luca, so you need to do your bit too. Do everything Mum tells you and don't make everyone feel worse by crying. You're getting to be a big girl now. You don't see Luca crying, do you?"

Katy lowered her head and shook it slowly.

"That's my girl," Dad said, hugging her. "It won't be forever. I'll figure something else out later on, but for now, that's the way it's got to be."

The next morning when we got up for school, he was gone. Mum was quiet, and Katy and I bolted down our breakfast, stuffed our lunchboxes in our bags and left.

School was about a 30-minute walk down the road. Dad had promised us a bike each for our birthday, but for now we walked. I was desperate for a bike. I already knew how to ride from trying other kids' bikes, but Dad said we needed to be eight first because then we'd be old enough to remember to be careful on the roads. There wasn't much traffic, really, but when the trucks came through, carrying sheep or machinery, they would thunder through, only slowing down when they veered off onto the side road that bypassed the town and then curving back onto the main road once it was past. No one had thought to take that road as far as the school, so it could be a scary place to be when a truck hurtled through.

The road was only gravel, and it was easy to skid, so all the kids knew to jump off their bikes and push them right off to the side into the dirt when they heard a truck coming. Other smaller roads joined the main one on the way to school, so Katy and I would only walk for a minute or two before other kids would come down those roads and join us. Some walked, some rode bikes, and the truly envied ones were the kids who rode their own horses.

The O'Brien boys, all three of them, had a pony each. So did the McCaghs. The horses would be tied up to the fence under the trees at the back of the school, their saddles pulled off and slung under cover. They seemed quite content to munch away slowly at whatever grass they could reach or just stand there, one hind leg bent up slightly and resting up on the hoof with their eyes glazed, until the school day was done.

The school only had 22 kids. Grades one to seven, all of us, were in the one room. A lot of the rich farmers sent their kids off to the city to boarding school when they'd finished primary school, but for now, we were all together.

"The days are long gone when you could just go and work on the farm at 14, boys," Mr Evans would say. "Farms don't just need labourers now; they need someone who knows business, who can do other things besides shear sheep and sit on a tractor. You need to be educated, or you'll go under. And as far as you girls go, you'll need an education, or the best you'll do is a job behind a counter in Coles in Geraldton and a bunch of kids."

The girls would always look at each other and sneer at this. They all wanted to get to Perth as quickly as they could. The smart ones were aiming for university or apprenticeships. As for me, I was too little to think about it much, but I knew I just wanted to work with Dad.

The day Dad started his new job always sticks in my memory for another reason too. One of my friends, Gary Morgan, was walking home with me. Katy was in a little group of girls a few metres behind us. It was a stifling hot day, the sun soaking through our clothes and skin in a way that, for some reason I could never fathom, caused little shivers to go through us every now and then. The wheat in the paddocks on either side of the road had been harvested, and although no breath of air touched us, we could see the wind sliding through the stubble, changing the flat gold to a rippling wave of silk.

As we plodded along, too hot to say much, we heard the familiar rumble of a truck from behind us. I turned and saw Katy and her group move onto the scrubby ground next to the road, and Gary stepped in behind me.

"I think it's a sheep truck," he said, as the roar of the truck got closer. He said something else, but I couldn't hear him clearly, not just because of the noise but also because he had turned away from me to look at the truck, which was only a few metres from us now. It passed with a flurry of dust from the gravel road, and I turned away, holding my breath. As the sound faded, I heard the girls behind me running and making 'panicky girl' sounds. I turned.

Gary was lying on the road, with his hands covering his eyes. His mouth formed a ragged 'O' that looked almost funny, and the most hideous sound roared from his throat. Blood gushed from between his fingers. The girls around us started whimpering, and I stood frozen, unable to think or move. The guttural screams from Gary slowed to a wheezy, gasping whine.

"What'll we do, Luca?" Katy pulled on my arm, and I woke from my fright.

"Run quick to Criddles and tell them to ring an ambulance, and then run home and tell Mum what's happened. She'll find Gary's mum."

Katy turned and raced off, her pigtails flying. The others ran off after her like a twittering flock of birds, leaving just me and Gary, the sun still beating down on us, silence only broken by Gary's rasping shudders. I patted Gary's leg in a useless and helpless way.

"You'll be okay, Gary. Someone'll be here soon." Gary's hand dropped from his face. He must have lost consciousness, and I could see a gaping bloody mess where his eye had been. A gravel stone, flicked up by the speeding truck, must have hit him. I sat there in the dust and heat, savagely brushing flies away from his face. I was crying loudly, but no one was there to hear me. They'd taken my dad away from me, and now they'd taken Gary's eye.

"Bloody trucks!" I blubbered. "Bloody trucks!"

off, my heart thudding. There was a long silence, and Mr Khan frowned thoughtfully.

"Yours is an interesting case. If only you had said something at your hearing in your own defence. As it was, a decision was made based on the evidence alone." He paused. "And that evidence was very damning. You rang the police and confessed to what you had done and then didn't speak again. The only witness was your sister, and she said very little too, apart from confirming what you had said." My heart pounded even more at the mention of Katy, but I silently counted slower and slower until it thumped more quietly.

I studied the desk. It looked expensive, maybe an antique, and oak, I think—no, darker than that, maybe mahogany—with a dark-green leather inset on the top and gilt leaves embossed around the border. Dad would have liked it. He used to always show me the different grains and patterns in different types of wood. I studied that pattern, counting every leaf, willing my mind to calm down and get back under control.

"Is there anything you want to say to me now?" Mr Khan asked, his eyebrows raised and his dark eyes never leaving my face. My face twisted in a wry grin.

CHAPTER FOUR

I woke early this morning and lay there thinking about Katy. I hadn't seen her since that last day in court. I hadn't heard from her at all. Where was she? Who was looking after her? There was no one I could ask. We'd never been away from each other for more than a night or two when we'd stayed at friends' houses. It was bad enough not having her around the corner let alone not speaking to her for so long.

I eat all my meals with everyone else now. I've tried not to, but I can't help but look forward to those three meals a day. Yesterday, after I finished breakfast, the guard said to me, "Come with me. The boss wants to speak to you."

I looked up, surprised. "Why?"

"No idea, mate, but on your feet."

"Okay, Mr Owen, I'm coming," I said, brushing my hair down quickly.

He laughed. "It's just 'Owen', not 'Mr Owen'. Owen is my first name."

I realised then that the staff here wouldn't want any of us to know their surnames. Too easy to track them down and cause trouble later on if anyone had a grudge. Using an adult's first name seemed friendly, but nothing here is as it seems. Owen stood outside the door again, and I stepped out in front of him.

"Go straight down the steps and then turn left."

I walked down the steps, conscious that he was right behind me. What did he think I was going to do? Throw myself head-first down the stairs and finish myself off? I turned and walked straight towards a double door. He stepped to one side and entered the code, and the door opened. I blinked in surprise. A long passage opened in front of me, and on either side were windows into large, well-lit rooms.

As I walked along, I could see that each room was a classroom of sorts. About 12 boys were in each room. I didn't have time to see what they were doing. In some rooms, they seemed clustered around a teacher; in others, they were sitting at desks or working at benches. Passing several guards, Owen quickened the pace behind me, and I could feel his hand on the small of my back.

"Step it up," he said, "Mr Khan is waiting." We came to the end of the passage, and then he stepped past me and knocked on a door.

"Come in," a voice called. Owen opened the door and motioned me inside. I stepped in, my eyes directly on the man in front of me. Mr Khan was only about my height. He was Indian-looking and dressed in a dark-grey suit, white shirt and tie. He stepped lightly and quickly around the desk, his hand outstretched.

"Hullo, Luca. My name is Abraham Khan. I'm pleased to meet you." He pulled a wry face. "Although I'm sure you're not too pleased to meet me under the circumstances."

His hand was warm and firm. Something in my belly clenched with a kind of shock, and he looked me straight in the eyes. How long it seemed since someone had touched me in a friendly way! I kept my face impassive, however, and he released my hand. Motioning to a chair, he sat down behind his desk.

"I know how difficult it must be for you to get used to this place—its rules, its loneliness—and, given the nature of the crime that got you here in the first place, you'll be here until you're 18." He paused and looked at me for a long moment. Despite my effort to not react to anything or anyone, I heard my voice break the silence.

"I know. They told me I would be here till I was 18 and then I'd be transferred to an adult prison."

He looked down at his desk, a small frown line between his eyes. "Yes. That means you will be here for just over two years. Your 16th birthday is…" he glanced down at a file, "July 30th! Very soon!" He smiled.

I felt a wave of annoyance. Big deal. Of what importance were birthdays in here except to mark another year out of my life, another year I'd been locked up like a dog?

"I know what you must be thinking."

My head jerked up. How could he know? He got to walk out those doors every night to his home, his family, his life. But then—he hadn't taken anyone else's life. He hadn't done anything so bad that he needed to be shut away from ordinary people. Hell, if I'd been a few years older and living in an earlier time, I'd be swinging on the end of a rope by now.

"You feel angry, lost and … hopeless." Mr Khan's warm, brown eyes fastened onto mine. My eyes filled suddenly with hot tears. In a panic, I chomped down hard on the inside of my cheek to stop them. It was the way he'd looked at me: sympathetic, kindly and almost loving. It wasn't so much what he said but that he actually

34

wanted to see past the monster boy to the person behind the shell I had formed around myself. I drew a quick, shuddering breath and looked back at him, a little more under control now that I could taste blood.

Mr Khan went on. "This can be a rapid learning time for you, Luca. Even though you feel cut off from everything you know and love, there is a lot of progress that can be made by you, even within the confines of these walls."

I frowned instinctively. What the hell was he talking about? He glanced down at the file again. "Your teachers at your high school have all commended you highly, particularly in science and maths, and they all commented on your maturity and intelligence beyond your years—although one teacher acknowledged that it was clear that you were not particularly happy but showed no inclination to let on to her what the problem was."

That must have been Ms Lake, my English teacher. She had asked me a couple of times to stay behind after class and talk—if I wanted to—about anything that was worrying me, but I had just said that I was fine, and she'd left it at that. I felt exposed—as though a spotlight were on me—just as I'd felt in the courtroom, and I squirmed involuntarily.

"We have excellent teachers here. They are very dedicated and used to dealing with all levels of problems. You've missed quite a lot of school over the past weeks, so you'll be starting again on Monday. I've put you in a class that may be at a lower level than your old class, but you have some catching up to do. The teacher, Mrs Shiels, will assess you and let me know if and when you are ready to go into a higher level." Mr Khan paused and leaned back in his chair. "But that's not the only sort of progress I'm talking about. The time you have alone and also with the other boys, many with severe problems, may help you come to understand yourself as well as others. You may develop compassion for them as well as for yourself."

I looked down, and a wave of annoyance flickered through me. "What's the point of any of it? I'd still be locked up. I won't be able to actually do anything in the real world no matter how much I learn."

"You may not always be in prison, Luca. There is always hope."

Sneering a little, despite myself, I said, "There was no time set on how long I was to be locked up. I know that I'm here for another two years, and then I go to the men's prison and God knows how long I'll be there for—probably till I die." My voice cracked and trailed

He smiled ruefully back. "Yes, well, I guess if you stayed silent in spite of all the questioning, you're hardly going to confide in a stranger now, are you?" He drew a long breath and then said, "You're not quite 16 yet, Luca. The law doesn't view crimes by minors in the same way it does crimes by adults. Of course, you must be here, and later in an adult facility, because of the nature of your crime, but it doesn't mean you'll be locked up for life."

I turned away from those dark eyes. "I killed two people. I won't be going anywhere for a long time; I know that much. I can understand you're trying to give me hope so I'll act like a model prisoner and not cause any trouble, but you're wasting your time on me," I said.

"Have it your own way for now, but you need to start learning again and mixing with the others more. You've needed some time to settle in, but there's a lot you can do while you're in here to prepare for life afterwards." Mr Khan glanced at me quickly. "You'll be spending more time with the other boys. There are sports and hobbies available. You've been under observation here since you arrived. That's why you've been alone so much. You've behaved well so far." He straightened the papers in the file—my file—and closed it dismissively. "Of course, if that changes in any way, those privileges will cease. Usually, a case manager is assigned to every boy in here. There seems little point in that while you are so unwilling to talk. We'll review that situation as we go."

He stood. There was no warm look in his eyes now. Probably I hadn't responded quite in the way he intended. I looked as disinterestedly as I could at the bookcase behind his desk, my eyes no longer meeting his. I glanced over the titles I could make out. They all dealt with juvenile crime. A bit one-dimensional, the old Mr Khan. The interview was over. Mr Khan's smile seemed a little forced as he said, "I'll speak with you again in a week or two, Luca." Then he nodded at Owen, who opened the door behind me. I stood and walked ahead of him without speaking. I just wanted to get back to my room to go over all of this and get back to feeling in control of myself again, away from people.

CHAPTER FIVE

Dad was away for a month before he came home the first time. Mum had told me he'd be there by the time we got home from school, but part of me didn't really believe her. Nothing had seemed right since he'd gone. It was like he, Mum, me and Katy were four parts of a machine that belonged together, worked together. With one part gone, we just didn't work. It was like we were holding our breaths; real life had somehow stopped—for me anyway. Mum hardly spoke to us. We'd drift in after school through the wire door, letting it slam as always, but she never called out, "You kids have a good day?" More and more often, she just looked up and said, "Say hello to Mrs Brockman."

Alma Brockman was always there now. Neither Katy nor I liked her. She was tall and kind of hefty with big arms covered in pale-orange freckles. Those arms were leaning on the table where Dad always sat, a pot of tea and Mum's best cup and saucer in front of them.

Mrs Brockman turned to look at us and smiled in that corny, fake way some adults do when they're talking to kids. "Hi, kids. How do you like being the man of the house, Luca?" She laughed without waiting for me to answer, lips peeled back, showing small, even teeth covered by too much gum. Crossing her fat, freckly legs awkwardly in her tight skirt, Mrs Brockman turned back to Mum and said, "Well, then he said…" and we took the chance to grab a couple of apples and headed to our room.

"Can't stand her," said Katy when the door was closed, and she started strutting around the room as though she had on heels that were too high and a very tight skirt. We both laughed, and Katy farted, a querulous *brrrp* of a sound that sent the pair of us into screams of laughter punctuated by long, silent painful gasps. I flopped onto the floor, holding my stomach till I could control myself. How can such a basic function never fail to get the same response even though we've heard it hundreds of times?

We sat there in silence for a while, and then I blurted out, "I hate it without Dad here!"

She put her hand on my arm and rubbed it. "I'm getting used to it. Dad doesn't really talk as much to me as he does you."

A pang of guilty delight swept over me. It was true. Although I wished sometimes that Dad would throw me around and tickle me like he did Katy, I wouldn't have swapped that for the things we did together, the things he talked to me about. He never would have talked down to me like Mrs Brockman had just done.

"Mum talks to you a lot though," I mumbled.

She nodded, smiling a little, and then she lay down next to me on the floor, still sighing now and then from her attack of laughter. Her smile made me see something I'd never seen before. In our little four-cornered machine, Dad and I were kind of paired, Katy and I were, Dad and Mum were, and Katy and Mum were—but not me and Mum. I loved her and she loved me, but not the same way she loved Katy or I loved Dad. It was hard for me to put into words, but I felt Dad's absence much more strongly then. I felt alone and rolled over and hugged Katy's back. She curved into my belly and chest automatically like we'd been doing since we'd been born, even before probably. I lay there, smelling her slightly musty hair, curving around her back, my top arm lying across her shoulders. How strange that we fitted together so comfortably even though she was a bit taller than me and quite a bit plumper. We even knew somehow when we needed to move, and we both changed positions at exactly the same time, reforming into another perfectly comfortable spot.

I'd slept with Mum once when I had tonsillitis and couldn't sleep. She'd come in with a glass of water in the dark and climbed in with me, but I'd lain there awake. Her knees had stuck into me, her arm had crushed me, and I was too hot. I'd listened to her even breathing, not wanting to hurt her feelings by getting out and going in with Katy, where I knew I'd be asleep in a second. I'd lain as still as I could till the birds started twittering in the trees outside and a pale grey line rimmed my blind, and then I'd fallen into a half-sleep, waking up groggy and bleary-eyed a couple of hours later. I could hear Mum in the kitchen, and I had stretched, relishing the space I had till it was time for breakfast.

We heard the wire door swing out and women's raised voices coming from the kitchen. "See you, love," said Mrs Brockman. "Thanks for the cuppa."

"Thanks for the company," Mum said, and as soon as we heard the front gate close, we knew it was safe to get up and go into the kitchen. Mum came back in, her face serious, a little crease running deep between her eyebrows.

"She's yucky, Mum," said Katy from behind the fridge, where she was rummaging for another apple. "Why doesn't she stay at her own place?"

Mum frowned, the crease deepening. "Don't speak like that, Katy. She's a very nice lady, and she keeps me company."

"But she's here nearly every day, Mum," I whined, something I knew she hated but it was too late to take back.

"Well, I'm lonely every day!" Mum snapped. "Now get out from under my feet and go and do something constructive, or I'll find you something to do."

We both turned and bolted, Katy to her room and me to the shed. The shed was cool and dim and creaked constantly in the heat, like an old man trying to get comfortable. Even though Dad wasn't there, I still felt good surrounded by all of his things. It made me feel like he'd be back soon and life would be normal again. I pulled out a few old sugar bags from under the bench and lay down. I could hear some bees droning away in the wattle tree outside, and I drifted off comfortably, thinking of how Dad would be home in a few days, and slept.

Saturday came, and I woke early. I slid my feet out from under my blankets, and they hit the linoleum floor. It was cold! But I pushed the blankets off and dressed quickly, tiptoed through the house, and unlocked the front door. Then I was running across the grass, wet and tickly, down the road, my breath following in smoky drifts.

The sun was nearly up. I loved this time of day, although I'd often wondered what the difference was between dawn and dusk. The sky would be streaked with the same colours, and the shadows would be long. Only the birds gave it away. The mudlarks were carolling, the roosters were crowing—answering one another as though saying, "I hear you!"—and swallows rolled and flipped through the sky like fish in the sea.

But now wasn't the time to think about all of that— Dad would be home soon. I kept running till I hit the school, and then I sat on the fence, scanning the horizon for any sign of dust, my ears pulled back with the effort of listening for the faraway rumble of the truck. The sun climbed, the dew seeming to be sucked up by its rays, and it began to get hotter. I don't know how long I sat there, half-dozing in the warmth yet alert in another part of my brain, and then I heard what I had been waiting for—the faint hum of a truck, travelling fast.

Jumping down, I ran to the middle of the road. Sure enough, I could see a faint cloud of orange dust, and the low drone of the truck was becoming higher in pitch as it got closer. I climbed onto the top of a fence-post, where I knew I would stand out and Dad would see me.

And then he was there, the truck's bellow deepening as he changed through the gears to slow down. It came to a halt in a long flurry of gravel and dust, and then there was silence apart from a ticking noise as the truck cooled down. The door swung open, and Dad smiled down at me, his eyes hollow and tired, and I leapt off the post and clambered inside the hot, smelly cabin. Dad's arms were around me, and I buried my face into his khaki, sweat-stained shirt. Ah, the smell of Dad. Everything felt right again, in place.

We drove home, me chattering away, asking questions, unable to shut up. He laughed at me and said, "Slow down, mate; my ears are falling off."

I grinned up at him, and we pulled up outside the front fence. Mum and Katy were waiting there, and Katy bounded out, but Mum just stood there with her arms wrapped around her. Dad swung

Katy up on one arm, and I hung onto the other, and he stumbled, laughing, towards Mum. She smiled, turned and walked back through the front door, and by the time the lumbering beast that was Dad, me and Katy arrived in the kitchen, she had the kettle on and biscuits on the table. Dad sat down laughing, pushing us both away.

"You're worse than blowflies, you two. Buzz off for a minute and let me say hello to your mum. Just wait here for a sec first, though; I've got to get something out of the truck." He was back in a minute or two, a little grin at one corner of his mouth. "There's a bit of rubbish on the front lawn. Could you kids pick it up?"

We dragged up the passage, unhappy at being dismissed so quickly, and then Katy gave a squeal.

"Luca, look!" There, leaning against the fence, were two bikes, both Malvern Stars—a red one and a blue one. That's the one time I really remember Dad coming home happy.

After that, even though I always waited for him and rode home in the truck, it was only good till we pulled up outside the gate, and Dad would just sit there for a minute, looking tired and sad. I'd say, "Are you ready now, Dad?" and he'd smile at me, and we'd go in. I don't really remember many of those times—everything's a bit of a blur: school, waiting for Dad, feeling a bit left out of things with Katy and Mum. Somehow when Dad *was* there, I felt that things had changed in a way I couldn't really work out.

During that time—I suppose over the course of about a year—I came to see that we weren't really the single unit I'd thought we were. Katy and I were pretty much the same—although she was loving having Mum to herself, and they spent a lot of time together—but for the first time in my life, I could see that Dad and Mum weren't really connected any more. Somewhere along the line, they had started to exist as totally separate people, and though I couldn't put it into words then, I remember feeling as though the solid ground under my feet had some cracks in it and they were somehow greatest between my parents.

I need to stop now. The next part I see as the beginning of the end. Just thinking about it starts my chest tightening.

CHAPTER SIX

On Saturday, instead of going back to my room after breakfast, a guard leads us past all the rooms and into a large gym. Archie comes alongside of me, his face split in his easy grin.

"So what ya good at, Luca? Footy? Basketball? Soccer?"

I had decided to keep my head down and keep to myself, but I can't help myself—Christ, I'm weak. "Nothing much, Archie. I'm a bit of a short-arse and I'm skinny too, so I never was much good at sport. I like to run, though."

I stop short. Early morning dew on the grass, everything sweet and fresh, pulling on my old running shoes and just going for a run, jogging down the road past all those silent houses—lazy slobs in their fusty beds, everyone asleep but me and the birds. Jogging off the slip of gravel, carefully over the top rung of barbed wire and into the paddock, my shoes sinking slightly into the rich loam of the firebreak, and then off I'd go around the edge of the paddock, past the wheat—sometimes just green spikes above the surface, other times stiff and straight, and best of all, golden and waving. Around I'd go, one full circuit when I was about 11, but then an extra lap every six months, and after that, I'd time myself from one corner of the paddock to the next.

Katy knew I snuck out early, and one day, she'd said to me, "Wake me in the mornings, Luca, and I'll come too."

It had only taken a half-breath of hesitation and she'd quickly jumped in with, "Oh no, don't worry. It'd be too early for me." She'd smiled to me, her freckled nose twitching, and I'd felt bad—but those runs were my time, just me and the earth and the sky. I couldn't share them, not even with her.

Now, here, in this high-roofed, crowded building that I can't escape, the urge to run, to be outside, is so strong that I wince. Archie sees it and looks away for a second. "Bet you want to be out there running again, don't you."

I nod quickly, unable to meet his eyes.

"I know what it's like. Not the running bit—just being out in the bush, the dirt under your feet, the sun

50

on your back… where you belong." His voice trails off, and I look at him then. His eyes are half-closed as though he is in a dream, but the sadness in them! He shakes his shaggy head, and his grin reappears. "Don't think about that now. There's a bit of athletics, so you can run if you want to, but they seem to go for team sports here. You should try footy. You may be a bit small, but if you're quick, you might make a good rover."

"Is that what you play?"

"Yeah, I love it."

I look at his broad chest with a twinge of envy. "You didn't get those muscles kicking a football around."

"That's right. I got them in the gym. Hey, that's it!" he says, "Sign up for the gym. You work hard and you won't be skinny no more. When afternoon lockdown is finished, you get an hour to do some sport or extra work on anything you're doing in workshop. Most guys just slack off and watch television, but you can do a lot of work in a gym in an hour. And," he adds, lowering his voice, "no one gives you much shit in here if you look like you could flatten 'em."

"Maybe," I shrug.

His wry grin darts up one side of his face. "What's the matter, white boy? You got something better to do with your time?" He laughs, and I have to laugh with him. I have no control over much of my life in here, but maybe I can control my body.

A whistle blasts shrilly, and there is immediate silence. A short, muscular man with white, close-cropped hair stands on the stage at one end of the gym. "Right, boys. Drop and give me 20."

The boys step apart quickly then, almost as one, and begin doing push-ups. I'm a second or two behind, but soon I too, with muscles burning after long weeks of inactivity, am down on the floor. The white-haired man picks up the count a few seconds in. "Six, seven, eight."

I feel myself rising and lowering to his count, as though I am part of a strange inhaling and exhaling beast. At 20, we collapse, groaning and laughing, but the whistle blows again and there is an instantaneous hush.

"Petrilli, Adams, Pickett, Johns. Ten more. I saw you all slacking off."

They drop to the floor as the rest of the boys laugh and shout, "Slackers! Pussies!" They get to their feet, grinning and puffing, and fall back in place when they are done.

"Okay. Into your sports gear. Football teams to the oval. Basketballers onto the court. Anyone left over, stay here. Five minutes!"

The boys disappear through doors to the side—into change rooms, I guess—and then there is just me and five other boys. The short man walks towards us. It is an unusual walk. He must be 60, but he doesn't move like any 60-year-old I'd ever seen. I've seen old farmers climbing stiffly up onto tractors and trucks or leaning against fence posts and just generally moving slowly, but this man seems to bounce lightly from foot to foot as though the muscles in his legs are taut and ready for action. His whole body radiates health, from his pale blue eyes to his clear, ruddy face. I must be 45 years his junior, but still aching from the push-ups, I feel like the old man.

"Right, boys, a couple of laps of the oval and then meet me at the high jumps." The boys turn and leave, and I am alone. "Well, Luca, isn't it? I'm Mr Robinson, the sports coach. The boys call me Robbo. What sport do you like?"

"I like to run," I say, "but maybe I could have a go at football."

"Good. Join the boys and do a couple of laps and then come over to the bench where the footy team is. I think basketball might not be your sport—at the moment anyway. You might grow more inches. How old are you?"

"Sixteen next week."

"Mmmm. You've got a bit of growing to do yet. Unlike me!"

I laugh politely.

"Right. Grab your sports gear from the tubs in the change rooms and then join the boys for a run. Remember to grab a pair of footy boots too."

The boys are coming out of the doors now, and I push against the tide and find some gear, pull it on and hurry out through the big doors at the other side of the gym.

I'm out! It hadn't really registered that I would be out! Out in the sunshine! The smell of grass, the wide stretch of the sky after having been inside for all those weeks! I didn't know fresh air could smell so good. I stand there, the warmth of the sun soaking through my skin like a hug, my eyes drinking in the colours, the shapes, but mostly the light and space.

"Move on," says a gruff voice behind me. "Join your group." It is a guard.

I jog off without responding, following the path the small group of boys is taking. The joy! I can't help it. I don't deserve to feel good about anything ever again, but I feel like I've just been reborn, out of darkness and into the light. I feel... I feel... How can I explain it? I know. I feel alive. Every part of me tingling, heart racing, muscles pumping, lungs dragging in that beautiful, beautiful air.

Alive—everything they're not. I slow my pace, not just because that realisation has cast a shadow over me but because I'm so unfit. Those months of lying around on my bed have left me weak, and I pull up, gulping air, and Aaron catches me up.

"You run pretty well," he pants and runs past me. He runs with such grace. His legs are long and lightly muscled, and he moves so effortlessly, like he could go on for ever.

The rest of the boys are already in two teams and milling around, kicking the ball to one another. I take a seat on the end of a bench. I can see Mr Robinson—I think it'll be a long time before I can call him Robbo— and the five boys who were running lined up and jumping over a bar. Mr Robinson raises it before Aaron begins his run at it. Even at this distance, I can recognise that lovely, graceful lope. He's propelled by smooth springs, over the bar and back on his feet almost as soon as he touches the ground, leaping and shouting and punching the air, his whoop of victory drifting above the footy teams' chatter. The bench creaks beside me, and with shock, I see it's Mr

Owen—Owen, I mean—and he's sitting next to me even though there's room all the way along the bench.

"Nothing like a game of footy," he says, almost to himself, as the game begins.

I say nothing, and we sit silently, but after a while I'm not uncomfortable anymore, and I begin to watch the game in earnest. They're not bad! I can see that big boofhead Brown lumbering around, using his body as a battering ram to punch kids in the back and elbow them in the face whenever the ref's back is turned. What a shit. I can hear Owen breathing hard every time it happens, but he says nothing.

Despite myself, I can't help but cheer when Archie kicks a goal. He seems to be everywhere. If there's anything wrong with that team, it's that they rely on him too much. But who can blame them? His shiny brown legs streak off away from the pack, and he seems to have some instinct that lets him know exactly where to kick the ball even though he appears not to be looking at where it's aimed.

Archie's legs are long with muscular thighs but no obvious calf muscles at all, and yet they are so nimble! He's like a cat, able to change direction on a pinhead, and he dances around the fumbling Brown, snatching the ball and whipping it away. It's not like he's playing football; it's like he's a ballet dancer, leaping onto the backs and shoulders of the other team to effortlessly cradle the ball in his hands and then hitting the ground running till he's ready to kick—straight to another player or through the open jaws of the goals.

Owen says, "He's going to be a legend one day. The AFL teams will be frothing at the mouth to get him." He pauses. "Soon as he straightens himself out."

I say nothing, but then he asks me a direct question, so I have to answer. "So what do you play then, Luca?"

"I don't play anything much." I pause. "Archie thought I might be okay as a rover."

Owen nods slowly and then says, "I think he's dead right. I saw you run, and you're pretty quick. You'll be able to duck in, grab the ball and be away before they know what's hit 'em. Just keep away from the big, mean mongrels."

Something's happening on the ground, and the game has stopped. The boys are in a big knot in the middle. Owen blows a whistle and runs toward them. Several guards sprint from their spots around the oval and wade in, and the boys grudgingly get out of their way, craning to see what's going on. I can just see through the tangle of legs that three guards are on top of someone on the ground who is trying to get them off with such strength that they're heaving and slipping as though they're trying to hold down a calf for branding. Owen stands to one side, making a call on his mobile, and then two guards run out from the gym doors, carrying a stretcher.

I can't see anything as they push through the crowd, and then a boy is lifted onto the stretcher and they jog back towards the gym. I can't see the boy's face, but whoever he is, there is blood running down his neck. I can see a gory mess where there should have been an ear. What the hell?

They're gone, and I turn my attention back to the group. It's breaking up now, and guards are shepherding all the boys into small groups and then back to the gym. As they clear the ground, I see that the three guards are still holding someone down. He must be tiring now because as he lashes out with an arm or leg, a guard grabs the limb, and finally Owen steps forward to catch a flailing arm. They lift him clumsily and carry him towards me.

It's Brown, and I can hear him swearing at them, but as they turn to go towards the gym, he catches sight of me and grins. I gasp and shudder. His top four teeth have been filed into points, and blood is running down his chin. Owen glares at me.

"Get to the gym," he snarls, and I jog, shaken, ahead of them into the almost empty gymnasium. The guards inside have most of the boys in rows now, with a few stragglers still hurrying from the change rooms. They're disappearing back towards the cells. I grab my clothes from the lockers, peel off the sports things and dump them, and within three minutes, we're all back in our cells.

I wash my face and am surprised at the shakiness of my hands when I lie on my bed. What a morning! But that taste of having been outside is stronger than anything else that's happened today.

CHAPTER SEVEN

Dad kept working away, and though we had new carpets in the house and Mum bought a new washing machine and was planning a whole new kitchen, it didn't really seem to make her happy. In fact, the only time she really seemed her old self was when Mrs Brockman came over.

She'd send us kids outside 'to play', and they'd huddle together over cups of tea and biscuits and lower their voices and talk about… what? I wondered.

We were eleven now and really a bit past the 'to play' thing. Mucking around in the dirt with toy trucks didn't really cut it anymore, and though Katy and I still talked about things and felt good when we were around each other, something had changed a bit. I knew she loved it that she had Mum to herself now and she felt a bit guilty about that because she knew I didn't have Dad, but I also knew that her girlfriends were her main focus now.

We'd go outside sometimes and maybe walk down the road and talk a bit, but before long she'd say, "I might just nick over to Amy's and see if she's home. What are you going to do?"

"I'm fine," I'd say. "I'll find a few of the kids and kick the footy around for a while."

"Okay, good. See ya." And she'd be off, her hair bouncing up and down on her shoulders. She'd changed. Even the old chubby, round little body was changing. I saw, as she walked away from me, that her legs were longer and she was thinner around the middle, and I couldn't help noticing when she wore a T-shirt that she was growing tiny boobs. God, that was weird. Then she'd turn around and grin, calling to me, "Let's go for a swim later, Luca."

I'd answer, "Sure," feeling happy for some reason. No matter how different she was starting to look, she was still my old Katy. I'd jog up to the oval behind the school. There was always someone hanging around up there to muck around with.

A few months later, I came home from school and plonked down on the edge of the veranda to pull my muddy shoes off. Mum was pretty fussy about that new carpet of hers, and she seemed to get angry easily lately. I knocked the worst of the mud onto the ground, rubbed the rest off with an old towel kept on a nail for that purpose, dropped the shoes into the shoebox and pulled my clean runners on. I was in no hurry to go inside because I could hear Mrs Brockman's voice braying away inside. I leant back against the veranda post and closed my eyes. I felt pretty good. We had a new teacher who seemed to like me, and he was great.

Today, he'd said, "Right, everyone, gather around and I'll read you a story."

We'd groaned a bit—quietly, because we weren't too sure what the teacher's limits were yet—and Glen Jacobs had said, "We're Grade Six, sir, not little kids."

"And this is no story for little kids. It's got murder, blood, executions, witchcraft and war." He had us now. "Get comfortable."

We'd dived onto a pile of old beanbags in the corner, he'd pulled a beanbag out in front of us and we'd all wriggled down, and then he'd opened a book.

"The story I'm going to read you happened a long while ago in Scotland. I'll fill you in with bits of it and read other bits. The language is from those times, so it's a bit different to that of today, but you can handle it; you're bright kids."

We'd all felt the same, I think, when he said that: embarrassed but pleased, so pleased that we were having trouble keeping the grins off our faces. Old Mr Evans had only ever growled at us and told us how stupid we were.

"Well," the new teacher began, "there'd been a war, and three men were riding back across the cold, misty moors of Scotland. One was named Macbeth…" and he'd read on all afternoon, reading bits from the book and then explaining any puzzling words. It was cold outside that day, just like on that Scottish moor, and we'd sat there, leaning comfortably against one another, pulled into the spell those strange, magic words were weaving.

Three o'clock arrived, but no one moved a muscle. The new teacher stopped and raised an eyebrow, and we'd all urged indignantly, "Go on, sir. Doesn't matter about the time. You can't stop there."

He'd laughed, clearly delighted with our response.

"Great place to leave it! What I want you to do tonight… Let's see—whatever takes your fancy. Either draw a picture of the witches around the cauldron, making sure you include as many of the ingredients as you can remember, or if you'd rather write than draw, you can write about how you think this may end. I promise if you all do your homework, we'll read some more tomorrow."

We'd rolled clumsily out of our cocoon of beanbags and run out the door, shouting, "Thanks, sir," and, "See you tomorrow, sir!"

"Make sure you do your homework, Bevan," my friend Martin said to the slackest person in the class as we shoved through the door.

"No worries," he'd said, "I love drawing. Fancy not having to write a whole lot of crap for homework." And that was the best thing really: that a teacher had actually given us a choice, had actually realised that we too liked a bit of power in our lives.

I was half-drowsing there, on the veranda, with the drone of the women's voices lulling me almost to sleep, when suddenly I jerked wide-awake. I'd heard a man's laughter in the kitchen, and it wasn't Dad's. I pushed open the wire door, and the voices stopped. They were all looking at me when I came into the kitchen: Mum, looking so pretty and flushed from laughing; Mrs Brockman, her red slash of a mouth wide open and dotted with crumbs of Nice biscuits caught in the fine hairs around her lips; and a man with gingery-coloured hair and ruddy skin. That's all I took in before Mum said, "Ah, here he is. Luca, this is Mr Reid, Mrs Brockman's brother. Say hello."

There was something about the way she said it, the way

she was speaking to me but looking at him, the way she had her hand resting on his shoulder—I disliked him on sight. He'd smiled confidently at me, touching my mother's hand as he stood up and moved around the table, his hand outstretched to pat me on the shoulder or shake my hand, I don't know, but I flinched away. Having done it, I couldn't undo it, so I stood, hardly breathing at my action. I felt rather than saw that he had not moved at all, frozen in that confident move forward, sure that I would allow myself to be touched by him.

I turned and looked him full in the face. His mouth was pulled back into a half-smile now, his large white teeth bare, his green eyes bland and cold. I heard a sharp intake of air from my mother, and I knew I had embarrassed her. A pang went through me, not simply because I had hurt her in some way but because I knew something had changed. But what?

"Luca, what's wrong with you? How can you be so rude?" Mum blurted out. "Go to your room and see if you can find your manners."

I hurried from the kitchen and closed my bedroom door but not before hearing Mrs Brockman's voice.

"Don't worry about it, Sylvie. It's just his age. They can be rude little buggers, and it'll probably get worse before it gets better."

"But he's never like that," my mother broke in, her voice a little shaky.

"Don't worry about it. He'll be right as rain tomorrow."

Don't bet on it, I thought and closed my door.

That night, as we sat down for tea, Mum was still angry with me, but she didn't refer to what happened. Instead, she started chattering away.

"Mr Reid has come from Sydney. Mrs Brockman told him one of the new businesses in Geraldton was looking for staff, so he decided to move across here to be nearer to her now she's on her own."

Katy looked up from munching her chop. "Is he a mechanic like Dad?"

Mum's eyes flicked away. "No, he's an accountant. He's a professional."

"Isn't Dad a professional?" Katy mused, more interested in getting the last bit of meat from the bone.

"No," Mum said slowly, "Dad's a mechanic. He works with his hands, like a tradesman. A professional person usually works in an office and has a qualification from a university, a degree. He works with his head more than his hands."

I felt somehow that Mum was saying Mr Reid was cleverer than Dad just because he was in an office. "How about a doctor?" I piped up. "He's gone to university, but he wouldn't be much good if he couldn't work with his hands, would he? How could he set a broken bone or operate on someone?" I felt pleased with myself.

Mum sighed. "Yes, you're right, Luca. Anyway, you can ask him about the difference tonight. They're both coming over for tea."

Katy and I both groaned. Mum slapped her hand on the table.

"That's enough! I treat your friends well whenever they come over. Do the same to mine. You forget that I get very lonely."

"But Dad comes home when he can!" I protested. Mum regarded me coolly but said nothing.

Katy dropped her bone on the plate and said, "That was yum, Mum. What's for sweets?"

The moment was over. I wanted to say more, but I didn't really know what I was trying to say. We ate our tinned fruit and ice-cream, Katy chattering on about some birthday party she was going to on the weekend and Mum promising to take her to town and buy a new dress for her. I cleaned my plate and went to my room.

*

Ray Reid was a frequent visitor at our place now. Mrs Brockman didn't always come, but one Friday night, Mum said, "You two are old enough to be on your own for a few hours. I'm going out tonight with Mrs Brockman and Ray."

"Where to, Mum?" Katy asked.

"Just out for a few drinks and a meal. I won't be late. Just stay here. If there's any big problem, go and call Mr Woolhouse next door or just ring my mobile. I've bought pizza for your tea."

Those Friday nights became a regular thing. Mum would dress herself up, looking and smelling beautiful. She had this one dress Dad loved. It was black and fitted her tight—that's all I remember—but the first time I saw her go down the drive with Ray Reid, wearing that dress, all I could see was his big, freckled hand stretched out across her back. Mum, you were so happy.

Katy didn't seem to worry. She mostly got on Facebook on those nights, and I would read a bit or do some homework to take my mind off the waiting, always waiting for Dad to come home.

CHAPTER EIGHT

That life seems so long ago. Here, life has freed up for me a fair bit. After sport on Saturdays, we have lunch in the afternoon, we clean our rooms and wash our clothes, and then we can go to the common room, or rec room as most people call it. There are chess sets, scrabble boards and computers to use, and the first day I wander in with the group, and Archie comes over to me.

"How's it hangin', Luca? Come to the gym?"

I hesitate for a moment because I know that, next to Archie, I am a runt. Still, I nod and follow him through a door off the main room. There are weights, treadmills and some gymnastic equipment in there—quite a lot, really. There are three guards in there, which is more than I'm used to seeing in a small area, but they're pretty relaxed and stand chatting and lounging about, throwing a medicine ball to one another every now and then.

"Been in a gym before?" Archie asks. He's raising himself on a chin-up bar, his muscles taut across his stomach and his arms hinging powerfully up and down like it's easy.

"Not like this," I say.

He swings his body forward, letting go of the bar and landing lightly by my side. "Well, let's give you a few things to do. Build up your arms, strengthen your back and shoulders, toughen up your gut," he laughs, punching me lightly in the belly.

Fifteen minutes later, I have a piece of cardboard ripped from the back of an exercise book in the pocket of my track pants. On it, Archie has written me a program—so many lats, overhead curls, whatever. I go through it, watching furtively to see how the others do them. My muscles burn, but it feels good to punish my body, make it hurt. Even though some part of me has died because of what I've done, my body is alive. I would push it till it hurt, make it strong. My body would be a wall, a fortress that no one could get inside. The vision of those filed teeth ringed by that bloody, grinning mouth pulses through my mind. No one.

That night, we have pizza and a DVD! I can't believe it! I had imagined that being kept in my room for

70

most of the day would be how life was in a juvenile detention centre. I sit on a plastic chair, munching on my slab of pizza and waiting for the movie to start, and I say to Archie, "Is this how every Saturday night is?"

He looks at me, pausing mid-munch. "Yeah, pretty much. Sometimes weekends are crap because there isn't enough staff on. Maybe on holiday or sick or something, so if the numbers aren't there, they keep us locked up, no sport or anything. It sucks, but mostly it's like this. Sometimes there's some sort of group that comes and puts on a play or sings or something, but not often."

"Bloody hell! Not bad for prison."

He laughs at me, throwing his head back. "You dummy! Did you think this was Alcatraz or something? We're all juveniles here. They treat us pretty good. I guess they think we're still young enough to change."

He munches silently for a few minutes, and I look around the room. Boys are licking fingers, burping and laughing, their chatter good-natured. It could have been any canteen in any high school. Weren't we here to be punished?

As though he has read my thoughts, Archie says, "It's not like this is meant to be a terrible punishment;

71

it's more like retraining. As though we'd 'gone off the rails', as Mr Khan says, and needed to be guided back on them."

"That Brown kid would take a bit of guiding," I mutter, finishing the last bit of pizza. "He's an evil bastard. Why did he rip that kid's ear off?"

"Felt like it, maybe. Jimmy probably got the ball off him or bumped into him. Who knows?"

We're silent for a minute. "I hope he never tackles me," Archie says, more to himself than me.

"You could take him," I say quickly. "He's heavier than you, but you're quick and fit."

He shakes his head. "I dunno. The thing is I don't really like hurting people. He loves it. That's what makes the winner, I think. It's not how big you are as much as how willing you are to hurt the other guy."

A silence falls between us. Dad used to say much the same thing. It's an old saying, I think: 'It's not the size of the dog in the fight, it's the size of the fight in the dog.' I knew what it meant now. Archie, for all his muscles, was somehow gentle. I sit there as the lights go off and the movie starts. I want to get tough and strong quickly, not for myself so much, but I'd hate to see Archie hurt. He was being kind to me. Sure, he doesn't know what I'd done—he might not want to be so kind then—but he made me feel human again, a little bit anyway, even though I didn't deserve it.

*

Sunday mornings are pretty relaxed even though we have to get up at the same time as we do the rest of the week. The time is pretty much our own, and as long as we're doing something productive, the guards keep a pretty low presence. Some kids play cricket if there're enough guards on duty to supervise; others stay in the rec room and read or play board games or table tennis. I go through the program again in the gym, but my muscles are screaming from yesterday. There are church services for the kids who want to go, but I keep well away. Not for me.

It's also visiting day. After lunch, all the kids line up to see their families or friends. They're hyped up, looking neater than usual, hopping around, keen to get through those doors and see who's waiting for them. I go back to my cell and lay on my bed. That panicky feeling I'd had in the courtroom is back, that nightmare feeling like I'm falling into a pit. *No one to visit you*, I think. Father long gone, mother gone forever, sister— silent. I turn over and face the wall. Why'd you have to get in the way, Mum? If only you'd kept out of it! I clasp my arms over my head, close my eyes and sleep.

After breakfast Monday morning, Owen taps me on the shoulder as we file out of the dining hall. "School starts for you today, mate. I'll take you to your class in 10 minutes. Get cleaned up and wait in your cell."

Fifteen minutes later, I'm walking down that corridor again, the one with the windows into classrooms on each side. I can see Mr Khan's door, but we turn left there and keep going. Owen stops in front of an open door and taps on it. Inside, a middle-aged woman stops what she's doing and smiles at us.

"New student for you, Mrs S," Owen says.

"Thanks, Owen."

Owen saunters off up the corridor and sits down on a bench where I can see two more guards deep in conversation.

"Come in, come in," the woman says, pushing back the steel-grey frizz that is her hair. "I've been expecting you, Luca. Mr Khan told me about you. I'm Mrs Shiels."

My eyes flicker up at her. So she knows too. All about me, what I've done, what a monster I am. Ah well, what's it really matter? Did I think it would be a big secret?

She points to a desk halfway up the first row. "There you go. I'll talk to you a bit later. Boys, this is Luca." A dozen pairs of eyes swivel to check me out. I know most of the faces, and I nod to them quickly and sit down.

"We've just started reading a story. Neil, could you fill Luca in on what's happened so far?"

I know without looking which person it is, but I turn in my seat and there he is, grinning at me, those pointed teeth zigzagging across his bottom lip.

"I'll fill him in, Miss," he says, "fill his face in with my fist." He laughs hoarsely at his joke, and several boys bray along.

Mrs Shiels waits till they finish. Silence. Her eyes never leave Neil Brown's face. He looks away uncomfortably. The silence stretches on, and finally she says, "Sam, perhaps you could answer seeing as Neil is being a smart-arse today."

The class laughs and even I do too. It's just so unexpected.

"Um, it's about this dude in Alaska who thinks he knows everything about the place even though he's from the city. He decides to tramp off with his dogsled into the snow even though everyone tells him not to, that it's much too cold..." While Sam is speaking, Mrs

Shiels moves towards Brown and speaks quietly to him, rubbing him on his big, spiky head. I look at that face, ugly sod that he is; he's smiling, those fangs making him look like a demented Rottweiler. I look more closely at this woman who has reduced him to a compliant lapdog.

"That about sums it up," Mrs Shiels smiles. "Well done, Sam." She's perched on the table at the front like a chook fluffing itself up for the night, her broad hips spreading out over its surface. Her legs are short and stumpy in their dark-blue slacks and don't even touch the ground. Her flowing white shirt adds to that chook-like appearance. She opens the book and begins to read. I keep studying her, but pretty soon I'm listening to the story. Though it's not cold in the room, the description in the story seems to make the temperature drop.

This poor idiot goes off on his own in the Yukon and makes one mistake after another till he freezes to death. But by the way this guy—Jack London, it says on the cover—writes, it's the weather that's the real story. When Mrs Shiels finishes, the boys talk about it for a bit, and then she sets them all to work and motions me up the front.

"I have some books here for you, Luca. I'd like you

to have a go at the maths and science ones later in your room and just flick through till you come to things you haven't learned before. Let me know tomorrow how far you got, and we'll see how much work you need to do to catch up. Don't worry if you don't get too far. From what your file says, you're a bright boy."

Yeah, right, real bright, I think. You have to be a genius to end up in juvenile detention, to kill.

I look down at the books that she's handed to me, and she adds, "Oh, I've got some files and paper and pens for you—the stuff you need for class." She pauses and says very low, so only I can hear, "Life *will* get better for you."

I take the books and box of stuff and turn and walk a bit unsteadily back to my desk. Christ, it's not being treated badly that I'm afraid of—I deserve it; it's kindness that I can't handle.

I keep my head down for the rest of the day, which passes quickly. I've been out of school for quite a while now, and I didn't realise how much I missed it. The class isn't too quick on the uptake generally, but Mrs Shiels teaches well. She explains things clearly and has interesting stuff for those of us who get it to go on with while she goes over things with those who don't. I notice the boys seem quite comfortable asking her for help. Strangely, they don't sling off at one another for being dumb, and some of the smarter kids wander over and help the others. The one called Sam comes over to my desk.

"Just give us a shout if you need a hand. I'm Sam."

"I'm Luca."

"I know. I'm not deaf. I heard her say your name," Sam grins.

"I'm not either. She said yours when she asked you to retell the story."

He pulls a wry face. "Yeah, well. See you around," and he wanders back to his seat.

I've only been here a while, but I've seen enough to know that there's a lot of viciousness around; not just the obvious sort like the chewed off ear, but something deeper, hiding, ready to leap out when the guards aren't looking or around a dark corner or in a lonely spot. But not in this room. It feels good—like a little island maybe—but around the edges I know the sharks are circling.

*

I drop my books on my bed and go to the gym for an hour, mindlessly going through the motions, and then I shower slowly. Some shift is happening inside me. Some tectonic plates of feeling are creaking out of their position, freeing themselves up slowly, and things are starting to flow again as they move. I dress and duck back to my cell. Usually, I'd hang around with Archie till he'd finished and we'd have our meal, but today enough was going on. I need calm.

I look at my cell with fresh eyes. It looks tidy but soulless, a room for a phantom or a dead man. Tipping the files, paper and pens out of the bag and onto my bed, I sit down next to it all and fish out the books Mrs Shiels had lent me. I'd never really read all that much before. There was a book by a Russian dude, *My Childhood*, plus a couple of oldies by Wilbur Smith and Leon Uris.

There's a study table fixed to the end wall, so I stack the books on it neatly. Next to that, I line up the files and then duck up to the kitchen and ask one of the kids on duty if he could give me a box of some sort. He disappears into the pantry room and comes back after a few minutes with a couple of small white cardboard containers.

I put one of the boxes next to the files and fill it neatly with pencils and pens. The other one, I stack underneath. It would do for the text books Mrs Shiels had given me. Pulling up the chair, I flick through one of the books—maths. The first couple of pages are pretty basic stuff I'd done last year, but then there is some graphing and algebra I've never done before.

I start reading the chapter and doing the exercises. I keep going like she'd told me, but it's no drag. It's really interesting. I'm understanding it! My brain is getting a real workout, and it feels good. I work my way through the whole book, and as I'm finishing the last page, the siren sounds for lights out. How quickly the time has gone! I push the chair out, stand up and stretch. I'm pretty stiff from sitting for so long, but I feel kind of powerful. My brain's cranking again. My body is waking up too.

Dropping to the patch of floor between my bed and the desk, I do a few slow push-ups. This is the way to survive: not to sit passively as I had been doing, waiting for my life to seep away—but to fill my time up. I'll build my body so it is as fit as it can be. And as for my mind, which never lets up, I'll give it plenty of work to do. All the time I sat there at my little desk tonight, not one thought of anything but understanding and solving those maths problems had filled my mind— nothing! I could control my thoughts through hard work—physical *and* mental. I could survive!

I feel so buoyed up that I could even, for now at least, forget that black hole that is inside me.

I climb into bed, and for a few minutes, I look at the desk, holding neatly lined up books, files and containers. It looks like home—not my old one as that was all gone forever—but this little home of mine where no one can touch me! I flick off the light, and for the first time in a long while, I fall straight into a deep, dreamless sleep.

CHAPTER NINE

Ray Reid as the occasional visitor didn't last too long. He seemed to be at our house every Friday night for tea. I just made myself scarce and stayed in my room or went over to someone else's place after tea. Katy always sat longer than I did. The three of them would talk away, so they really didn't seem to notice that I hardly ever said a word. If Ray spoke to me, I'd make sure I didn't make eye contact and I'd mumble the shortest reply I could. Thank God he gave up after a few weeks.

One night was really hot. I'd gone outside after the dishes were cleaned up. I lay on the sad bit of grass that Mum had watered earlier. It was a bit prickly, but the water on it cooled me down, and every little puff of wind sent a delicious little shiver through me. I looked up at the night sky. It looked like a huge upturned soup bowl, and I remembered how hard it had been for me to understand that the earth was actually round and not flat with a semi-circular lid. Dad and I had lain out there together one summer night like this, and he'd pointed out the different stars to me.

"Just think, Luca, your grandfather, his father, his father and so on—all the way back to the beginning of time—have looked up at those stars. Makes you think, doesn't it?"

I had lain there for a while, thinking about all those people who'd come before me. "Where do we go when we die, Dad?"

He hadn't answered for a while, and then he'd said, "Well, no one really knows for certain, but a lot of people think they do."

"What do you think?" I'd asked, slightly panicky. Dad knew everything, I'd thought, and this was an important question even if no one talked about it much. The thought of death as permanent darkness going on for ever and ever had terrified me.

He hadn't answered for a minute, and then he'd rolled onto one side and put his hand lightly on my chest. "I think that there's part of us that never dies. When we die, I think that part, which people call the soul, steps out. It's a bit like your old kindy clothes. Remember that Batman T-shirt you always wore?

83

Mum would try and get it off you to wash it, and you'd sneak it out of the basket!"

I'd laughed. "I know. I wanted to wear it everywhere, even to bed!"

"What happened to it?"

"It had a few little holes in it, and one day when I pulled it on, they joined up and it ripped right across the back."

"Then what?"

I had been stumped for a minute. "I felt sad, and then I threw it away"

"Exactly," he'd said. "Think of your body like that T-shirt. One day, it'll get old and damaged till it completely gives up and you'll step out of that old body and move on. You aren't your body, are you?"

This was a hard one. "Aren't I?"

"Point to the part of you that is *you*."

I had done a quick scan of my body. Not my legs or arms; they could be cut off and I'd still be me. "Maybe..." I'd said slowly, "maybe my head."

"Why are you your head?"

"That's where I think, so that's probably where I am."

"Not a bad thought, Luca. In fact, that's the place where all your thoughts are—but you're not your thoughts, are you?"

"No, I don't think so."

"Then what are you?" This was too hard. It seemed like a simple question, but I just couldn't answer it.

Dad had laughed. "Don't worry if you can't answer it now. It's the question we're all born to think about. Time for bed. We'll talk more another time." And we'd wandered back inside, brushing bits of grass off each other's backs, and I'd felt comforted but couldn't really work out why.

I lay there, thinking about this memory, when I felt Katy sit down next to me. "What are you thinking about?" she asked, lying back next to me and resting her head on her hands like I was doing.

"Nothing much. Maybe a bit about Dad."

She didn't say anything for a while, and then she said, "You're pretty rude to Ray, Luca."

"What do you mean? It's just that I don't hang off everything he says like you and Mum do."

"No, it's more than that. You hardly even answer him when he talks to you. He hasn't done anything to you."

"He shouldn't even be here!" I exploded. "He should have his shoes under his own table every night instead of having 'em under Dad's!"

"Well, Dad's hardly ever here!" Katy spat.

"That's not his fault," I shot back, rising to sit and face her. "He's away working for us, not having a fun holiday. How would you like to drive a truck all day and part of the night for days and days, unload, and turn around and do the same thing with more stuff every day of the week?"

"I know," she said, turning away from me. "I get that he works hard. But when he comes home, he's horrible. He's not like Dad at all. He hardly speaks to us, and he and Mum look like they can't stand each other."

There was no defence to this. What she said was true. "But Mr Ray Bloody Reid shouldn't be here just 'cos Dad can't be."

"Mum can have friends too, Luca. And he's really nice to me."

"Yeah, he buys you stuff."

She winced. "What's wrong with that? He's just being kind. Mum says because he's new here, he hasn't got many friends yet, and she's lonely on her own, so it's good for both of them. She's happy when he's around. She laughs like she used to."

"It's just wrong," I muttered, but I couldn't think of anything to say to convince her. I just knew something was horribly wrong and our little four-wheeled machine was heading for a crash.

Dad came home a few days later. It was a Saturday, and I hoped he'd come to Geraldton and watch the footy with me. I knew it was a long shot; he usually slept all day Saturday. I didn't get much of a chance to even mention it. Mum came out to the truck as he pulled up and waited for me and Katy to say hello to him, and then she moved forward and instead of saying hello to him too, she said, "Dan, we need to talk. You two leave us in peace."

Katy and I looked at each other, surprised, and then we looked at Dad's face, but it didn't look surprised; it looked mean and wary, not like I'd ever seen him before. We slunk off. I looked back once, but Mum and Dad had gone inside. Katy was silent, and I couldn't think of anything to say. Her hand reached across to mine at the same time mine reached out to hers. We hadn't done that in a while. We turned to each other with the same little smile on our faces and then burst out laughing as we realised that we must look like a mirror image.

"Come on!" I shouted. "Race you to the river!"

Katy squealed as I got a head start, and I heard her laughing and running behind me, both of us keen to be fossicking around the river for a couple of hours.

At that time of the year, it wasn't so much a river as

a stream, but it never completely dried up, although some years it was just a series of disconnected ponds. Huge old river gums thrust branches from one side to almost half-way across to the other, and we had climbed up and sat in the crooks of their splotched old arms. The bees were buzzing, and we lazily slapped at tiny ants that tickled our bare legs and arms as they dashed about. Neither of us said much. It felt so good there, and it wasn't till the sun had started sliding down behind the trees and turning their silvery trunks a dull pink and cool breezes were turning chilly that we slid down and headed for home.

It was quiet in the house. Usually Mum would be clattering around in the kitchen and getting tea ready at this time, but there was nothing. The door banged behind us, and we trailed down the dim passage. Mum and Dad were sitting at opposite ends of the table. Mum looked away as we walked in, but I saw that her face was red as though she'd been crying. She didn't look sad, though—just determined, her lips pressed tightly together.

Dad's face, on the other hand was white, and his eyes were sunken. I'd only seen him look like that once before. I guess it was when I was about eight, and he'd been called out to an accident at the crossroads on the way to Ellendale. He'd been gone a long time, and when he'd come back home, he'd had that same look on his face. He'd gone straight to his and Mum's bedroom, and we'd eaten tea alone.

"What's wrong with Dad?" I'd asked Mum.

"It was a bad accident, Luca. Maybe one of them didn't stop to give way to the other one or they'd been drinking, but it seems like the driver of one car and the passenger of the other were killed." Her voice had shaken a little. "That passenger was Daisy Farrell. You know, Mrs Farrell's daughter who works in the chemist shop."

"But she's only young!" I'd protested. Young people weren't meant to die! I'd tried to picture Daisy, and though I must have seen her heaps of times, all I could think of was her long, blonde hair and the way she laughed.

"I know. She was only seventeen. It's terrible." Mum's voice had cracked, and she'd put her face in her hands. "Poor Mr and Mrs Farrell. Dad went there to get the cars off the road so they wouldn't cause any more accidents. Just leave him be tonight."

That's how his face looked now. His hands were flat on the table—those blunt, square fingers always with a bit of black grease around the nails no matter how much he scrubbed them—and as Mum turned back towards us, I saw those hands tremble.

"Sit down, kids," Mum said quietly. We slid onto our chairs, and she took a deep breath. "Dad and I have been talking, and he's going to be going away."

"He always goes away," Katy said, her brow crinkled. "He has to drive the trucks."

Mum swallowed. "No, more than that, Katy. Dad isn't going to live here anymore."

I felt panic rising in my chest. I had my friends, school, running and Katy, but nothing was as important as having Dad here. Without him, we'd just grind to a halt like a car running out of petrol.

"But Dad," I protested, but he'd turned away from me.

"You're horrible, Dad!" Katy burst out. "You just like being away from us!" She ran to her room, slamming the door. I wished she hadn't done that. She was just making things worse.

"But where would you live?" I whispered.

He turned and looked at me. "I don't know, mate. I don't know anything. But it's what your mother wants, and it's what's going to happen."

"When will I get to see you, then?"

"Maybe not for a while. Let's just take things easy."

Pushing my chair back, I walked as steadily as I could to our room. I didn't want to cry or yell like Katy had. Round the corner I could hear her sniffing away, but I didn't want to comfort her or have anyone near me. I sat on the end of the bed and watched the light fade out of the room. Somewhere in that time, I heard Katy's breathing become deep and even, and then darkness fell. Still, I sat.

Finally, I got cold, sitting in the dark. I lay down, suddenly desperate for sleep, but I needed to go to the toilet. Inching the door open so they wouldn't hear me, I crept outside and piddled off the edge of the veranda into the lantana bush. The air was crisp, and the sky was that dark mix of blue and black just before night is completely here.

The front door light flicked on, and I pushed myself back against the wall into the shadows. Dad and Mum stood in the doorway. I could tell Mum was crying. "I don't know what to say, Dan," she said. "You've done nothing wrong. It's just finished; that's all. We're too far apart to get back again. It's been a long time coming…" Her voice trailed off.

There was a long silence, and I held my breath in case they could hear me. The crickets started up, and O'Brien's old kelpie started woofing away as he always did when the moon came up. Dad used to say he must have a bit of werewolf in him.

"That's your decision, Sylvie, but the kids…" His voice choked off, and I heard the door creak as though he'd leant against it.

"Maybe," Mum mumbled, "Luca could live with you. You know what you mean to him."

"No. How could you separate him and Katy? They're twins." Dad moved clumsily through the door. I could see he had a large case at his side. "I'll come past tomorrow and get the rest of my stuff when the kids are at school," he said, and then he stepped off the veranda awkwardly and out through the gate.

The light flicked on as he opened the truck door and heaved his case inside. He walked around the other side, his boots crunching the gravel, swung up into the driver's seat and the pulled the truck down the road. I stood there in the darkness, watching the red of his tail-lights growing smaller before he turned the corner and was gone. My ears strained, but within a minute, I could hear nothing—just the dog baying at the moon. Mum sighed, a long, shuddering sound and then switched off the light and went inside. I snuck in through the back door and slid into my bed.

A few minutes later, Mum pushed open the door

and stood, framed there, for a long time. I breathed as lightly as I could.

"Do you want some tea, Luca?" she whispered. I didn't answer. She must have known I was awake somehow, but I couldn't speak. She stepped back and closed the door, and soon after, I heard the shower running. Still no clear thoughts came to me, and I didn't want them to. This numb feeling was the best way to feel right now, I knew, and I hoped it would last for a long time.

I'd run home straight after school the next day, but no truck was out the front. Mum wasn't home either, and instinctively, I ran straight through the house and out the back to the shed. It was bare. The 44-gallon drum Dad used for rubbish was full of old offcuts of wood, bits of sandpaper and empty oil cans, but the shed was swept clean. My eyes grew accustomed to the dimness, and I saw a large wooden chest—Dad's grandfather's tool chest—which I knew had come from Italy. There was a large sign on it in Dad's writing that read: For Luca.

I opened the lid, and there, laid out neatly in rows, was a full set of tools, Dad's best ones—his screwdrivers, wrenches, hammers—the lot. The numb feeling was gone in a breath, and a sharp pain somewhere in my stomach doubled me over. I sank to my knees, the tears burning my eyes, my breath gasping. It was just the pain in my stomach. He was gone as suddenly and completely as that red brake light going around the corner, leaving only darkness.

I never saw Dad again. A card would arrive each birthday for both Katy and me with two $100 notes inside it, but that was it.

CHAPTER TEN

The next morning, I wake early and lie there, lifting my head a little and seeing the unfamiliar shapes of the boxes and books on my desk. My head drops back, and I smile. I feel different. I close my eyes and run over in my mind the maths I'd done last night. Yep. Still there. I want to do more, but I'd finished the book. I lie there comfortably, hearing the sounds start as the other boys wake. I'm up and dressed with my books on the end of the bed by the time the wake-up siren rings.

I hand the maths book to Mrs Shiels as I walk into the class.

"What's this, Luca? Too hard?"

"No, I've finished it."

"All of it?" Mrs Shiels shoots a sharp, disbelieving look at me. I nod, and she smiles. "Well, while the rest of us go on with the section we're up to, which is near the beginning, maybe you could do the test that covers the work done in the whole book." I sit down to wait while she organizes the rest of the kids and finds what she wants for me.

Sam comes over a few minutes after they start, "Give us a hand, will you, Luca?" He pulls his chair over. "I just keep getting these wrong. She explains them to me and it's clear, but when I come to do them on my own, I just get fouled up again." He laughs ruefully. "Bit thick maybe."

He's having trouble with graphing, so I get him to do some simple graphs using footy games and scores so he gets the basic idea, and then we start doing a few harder ones. Mrs Shiels wanders past a few times to see what we're doing but says nothing.

"They're not hard at all!" Sam says, after getting most of them right.

"Which means you're not thick after all." We laugh, and he says, "Thanks, mate," and goes back to his seat to begin working. Mrs Shiels comes up to me.

"Here's the test I'd like you to do, Luca. Have a go at all of them." I turn to take it from her and see Neil Brown's blank, cold eyes staring at me. I can't keep my lip from curling in contempt, and then I turn away and start to read. Everything is fresh in my mind, so

I find it pretty easy. Mrs Sheils takes my paper, and we all pack away for lunch.

As I walk out through the doorway, I feel a sharp pain in my ribs. Grunting, I swing around, straight into the broad chest of Brown. I jerk back from him, but he shoves against me so I'm pinned against the door jamb. He bends his head to my ear and whispers hoarsely, "Think you're smart, do you? You won't look so smart with your teeth rammed down your throat, will you?"

The guard outside in the passage appears next to me. "Move along, you two. Back to your cells."

Brown lurches off, twisting the heel of his shoe on my foot as he leaves. I slip my hand under my shirt and touch the spot where I felt the stab of pain. My fingers come back smeared with blood. Brown must have been carrying a razor or nail. I sit on my bed and pull my shirt up, and after I wipe the blood away, I see four puncture marks. I clean them up quickly and tape a folded hanky over them so the blood won't show.

At lunch, I ask as casually as I can, "Where's that Brown kid? He hasn't been at meals since Saturday."

"He's on regression for a month," says Archie through the hamburger he's munching. "He only comes out for classes. No sport, no rec, no anything. Not much of a punishment for ripping someone's ear half off, but it's great not to see his ugly mug spoiling our food."

"Nothing could spoil this," chirps Tim. "This is bloody beautiful." He grins at us, and we can't help but laugh at him. Apart from the mayo running down his chin, his teeth are festooned with ribbons of lettuce.

"You're a pig!" says Archie. "Shut your gob when you eat."

So begins my routine: breakfast, class, lunch, options, an hour back in the cells, tea, rec—or most nights for me, study. I keep to myself pretty much, apart from the boys at my table and Archie at the gym and at football training on the weekend.

Sam speaks to me in class sometimes, but the gap between what they are doing compared to where I am widens, so I tend to work alone. The only thing that breaks the routine during the week is rostered duty, which is only a few hours a week. We work in the kitchen, the dining room, the library or the gym. A few boys get to work in the garden and others in the infirmary, but it is a special privilege to work there. We do a block of six weeks and then move on—oh, and of course, the weekends.

There is sport on Saturday as long as there is enough staff available, or there is lockdown instead, rec for longer and visitors and church on Sunday. The month Brown is absent is great. It helps me see how important it is to keep to myself as much as possible. I confine myself to Archie, talking to him a bit when we are alone. As for the rest of the boys, I am nice enough, but I make it clear I have no interest in developing any friendships.

I keep my head down, keep out of trouble, and keep out of Brown's radar. That sharp stab to my ribs reminds me of how important it is to keep myself to myself. I want to ask Archie what had punctured my skin in that neat, four-pronged row, but I keep it to myself.

Never happened.

CHAPTER ELEVEN

There is one thing, though, better than all the rest. It makes it easier to keep to myself because it confirms that I'm not as alone as I thought I was.

The afternoon of my birthday, the day I turn 16, I find two envelopes on my desk. One has the centre's address printed on it. I open it, and there's a plain white card from "Mr Khan and all the staff", wishing me a happy birthday. I know they're probably churned out automatically by some computer, but it makes me feel good all the same. Trying to make the normal feel normal.

I remember something I'd heard something on television when I was watching a doco on Nazi Germany. It was the word Hitler had used for Jews, gypsies, homosexuals, criminals, and other so-called defectives: 'Untermensch'—the 'underpeople', the sub-humans—unable to function as they should and unable to fit in with the way society should work. All the cards in the world aren't going to change that. In another world, I'd be having a party tonight, but all that is over.

Picking up the other envelope, I see my name typed on the front. Probably from Mrs Shiels. I rip it open and pull out the card, and a photo drops onto my desk face-down. I flip the photo over and look blankly at it for what seems like a long time, and then realise I'm not breathing. I suck in a deep breath and pick up the photo, drinking it in.

It's a photo of Dad and me when I was about two. I'm in his arms, and it's a side-on shot. I have a hand on each of his cheeks as though turning his head to me, and he is looking back at me with as much intensity as I am looking at him. It's a fairly close shot, but I can see the corner of the shed in the background. Dad's hair is in a weird hairstyle—curly on top and long at the back—the old 80s mullet! But it's Dad.

The birthday card is still in my hand. On the front is a boy who looks vaguely like me with a car filled with blondes in a thought bubble above his head. "Happy 16th!" it says. Inside is a corny little poem, like there always is, but no writing. There's no "Dear Luca" and not even a signature—just the blank card. I look on the back of the card. Nothing there either.

It's Katy. It must be—there's no one else—but why didn't she write something? I close my eyes. I can hear the faint sounds of a television and a guard, heavy-footed, past my door. My eyes ping open, and I scramble for the envelope. There's nothing written on the back, but the front is postmarked Perth. What the heck's she doing there?

Then it hits me. I've been so numb through all of this that I haven't really thought about her. I haven't really thought about anyone but me. Where is she? I'd seen her in the courtroom, but I didn't know where she was living. Somewhere in the back of my mind, I just imagined her living at one of her friend's houses, still at school, life going on.

But of course that couldn't be true. I'd killed her mother and her stepfather. What was I thinking? Not thinking, more like it. Too caught up in what was happening to me to think about her. What sort of scum am I? That's why there was no message on the card. What is there to say? Why would she want to say anything? …Still, she'd sent me this! She thinks about me. I still exist out there.

Afternoon lockdown is nearly over. I usually read

in that time, but today I just lie on my bed, liking the feeling of being just a little bit happy.

*

Archie is in the gym before me, as usual. I go quickly through my routine, skipping a few repetitions, and then I sit on the bench at the side, watching Archie lift weights. He doesn't seem to sweat much, and the only sign of strain is the crease between his eyes. He glances across at me when he sits up, wipes his hands and bounces lightly, punching the air, and makes his way over to me, plonking himself down on the other end of the bench.

"Lazy today, bro?" he says.

"Birthday. Slacking off as a present to myself."

He raises his heavy eyebrows. "Happy birthday. Sweet 16 and never been screwed?"

I laugh, trying to make it sound like he's said something ridiculous rather than absolutely, tragically true, and Aaron wanders over. He's been on the bike, reading a book while he pedals. "What's the joke?"

"Luca's birthday."

Aaron grunts. "Guess we can rule out picking up a few chicks and getting shit-faced." We sit in silence

103

for a few moments, thinking, and then I pull up my shirt. They both look at my scabbed red dots and nod to each other.

"Get a bit too up-close and personal with the snake, did you?"

"How did you know it was him?"

"That's one of his little tricks. He picks up the ring pulls off the tops of cans and then he clips down the pull part till it's a sharp point. He does that to a few of them, lining up and sticking together the sharpened bits so they're strong, and then he opens up the ring part to fit over a finger. He puts one over each finger, and there you have it—prison knuckledusters. We've just about all felt them. They hurt like hell, and I guess they'd do real damage if he went for your eyes or throat, but he keeps it to where the guards won't see."

"Just keep away from him," Archie breaks in.

"I do!" I protest. "I don't know what I did to piss him off."

"You don't need to do anything," Aaron says. "You're new, so he's just letting you know he's Mr Tough Guy around here."

"Which is his cell?" I ask.

"He's four down from you, but he's not there at the moment. He's in Riley House."

"What's that?"

"It's like a sort of prison within a prison. Great, isn't it, Arch?" Aaron says. "They bring you into this place you're going to be stuck in for years, and they don't even bother to show you over it on the first day."

"You're so shit scared on the first day that you probably wouldn't take much in anyway."

"Still," Aaron goes on, "it's just basic decency, really."

Archie rolls his eyes at me. "He thinks he's in a flash private school here."

"No, I don't, but anyway, have a look next time you're on the oval. You'll see that the buildings are in three clusters or blocks. Each one has four wings, and there are eight cells in each wing. That's 32 of us in each cluster, so when it's full, there are 96 of us. They're just called Block A, B and C."

"And we're in A Block," I break in. I feel a bit stupid not having taken any notice or asked any questions about this before. My cell is 5A, so it's a fair guess.

"Yep, that's right. Apart from that, there is the gym—which you've seen—a rec room in each block and the infirmary, which is attached to Riley House."

"Which is…?" I prompt.

"It's like a solitary confinement-type setup. There are usually about two or three kids there, so it's not

105

really completely solitary. When you do something wrong, they take you over there and keep you apart from everyone else except for school. If you've done something really bad, you don't even get to come to class; you just do your work in your cell. It's isolation, really, but instead of calling it that, they call it regression, like you've gone backwards. Brown got regression for a month because of what he did to that kid's ear."

"Hope he doesn't regress any further. He's a Neanderthal now," I mutter darkly.

They both smile.

"What other things get you put in there?"

"Apart from assault, there's bullying—although the guards look the other way a lot of the time for that—and there's fighting, abusing the staff, doing drugs, smashing up the place... Anything else, Arch?"

"Mmm. Having a weapon. That's about it. Oh, yeah, the worst thing you can probably do is assault staff."

"What do they do in Riley House?"

"Loss of all privileges—like no TV, no rec, extra work, no sport and no pay."

I jerk my head back in surprise. "What pay?"

"Don't get too excited. You get just over three bucks a day while you're in here. Your family are only allowed

106

to give you $20 for your birthday or Christmas, no more, so you can use your account to buy stuff at the canteen."

"There's a canteen here?" I squeak. Wish my voice would hurry up and finish breaking.

"Yes," they both squeak and then slap each other on the back, laughing like fools. I can't help but laugh with them.

"Very funny," I say when they stop laughing and repeating the squeaky "yes". "Now where's the canteen?"

"Come on," Archie says, getting up from the bench. "It's only open for another 10 minutes. I'm not going to get anything done in here, so we may as well nick off."

The three of us leave the gym and walk to the end of the corridor, past my cell and around a corner. I do the calculations as we walk. Remand centre plus the time I've been in here at $3 a day… That's over $200!

"Do they pay you while you're in the remand centre?"

They both hoot with laughter at me. "You greedy bugger! Remand's just a holding pen. They can't give you an allowance as an inmate because you're not one yet."

Aaron nods in agreement. "Remand's kind of like

Limbo. You know, that place you go after you die where you wait to see if you're going to Heaven or Hell. Same concept. If you're set free—Heaven; this place—Hell."

Archie shrugs. "Only Limbo I ever heard of is where you dance under a stick and try not to touch it." His brow wrinkles. "Must be a bit hard for a girl with big tits. She'd fall flat on her back trying to get under the stick."

Aaron breaks in. "Any chick with big tits can fall flat on her back in front of me any time, don't you reckon, Luca?" We all laugh loudly like we really know what we're talking about—or more to the point, live in a world where there even *are* any girls.

There is a murmur ahead of us as Archie pushes a door open to the right side of the exit at the end. There are about a dozen boys crowded around a counter. There isn't much to choose from on the shelves at the back, but there are two fridges full of cans and bottles of cool drinks, a small ice-cream fridge and stacks of potato chips in a steel basket. Apart from that, there are some chocolates and a few rows of magazines and comics on the shelves. A couple of guards are laughing and chatting while an older boy I hadn't seen before is serving the boys and another boy is putting the stuff

108

on a computer. I figure I have a fair bit in the account they told me about even without any money while I was on remand, so I turn to Archie and Aaron and say, "What do you want? I'm buying."

They both look a bit stunned. "You don't have to do that."

"I want to," I cut in. "Just this once maybe, but I want to."

"I'll have a Coke," Archie says.

"Me too," grins Aaron.

I walk to the counter, and the boy flicks a look at me and asks my name. He taps it in, waits a few seconds and then says, "Yep. What'll it be?"

"Three Cokes and three packets of chips." I hand the goods to the boys, and we wander back down the corridor to the rec room. We sit in a corner and pull the tops off our cans, glugging for a few seconds. Aaron is the first to let out an almighty belch, and then Archie and I try to out-do him. We sit there munching and crunching, and just for minute, it's heaven. I don't think I'll ever enjoy knocking back a can of Coke as much as I am now.

"Happy birthday, mate," Aaron and Archie say, toasting me with their cans.

I find I can't answer. I nod and look away, and

luckily, the siren goes for clean-up before tea. I wave quickly and hurry back to my cell.

That night, as I lie in bed, I can't help but smile. Not such a bad birthday.

CHAPTER TWELVE

It's strange that, on the outside, nothing seemed to have changed when Dad left. Katy and I still walked to school each day, mucked around with our friends, did our schoolwork and walked home. Something was a bit strained between us, though. We chattered away—same as ever—finishing each other's sentences, but we carefully kept away from the subject of Dad.

As far as Mum went, I could see she looked happier. That hard, angry look had gone from her face. She and Katy were the same as ever, but with me, it felt like she was putting on an act. She was too bright and too chirpy around me, buying me new clothes and making my favourite food for tea. I smiled and thanked her, but it was all false. She'd blown my life apart for no good reason that I could see.

I started hanging out with my friends a lot more after school and on the weekends, and at night, I ate my tea as quickly as I could and then left the table, saying I had homework. I didn't, of course, but Mum never objected, and a few minutes later, I could hear her and Katy laughing away as though I somehow freed things up for them by leaving.

I pretty much did what I'm doing now, in a way, although in here, order is imposed on me; back then, I imposed it on myself—I made sure I filled every minute. The good bit was, I suppose, that all my grades improved. I'd always been okay at school, but after Dad left, in my room each night, I went over everything and even read ahead in my books so that when we came to that stuff in class, I already knew it.

Mr Squires asked me to stay back for a few minutes one day, and he said, "You're going great guns, Luca. Well done." I'd shrugged, embarrassed, and he'd put his hand on my shoulder. I looked up, surprised.

"Look, it may not be none of my business, but I've heard that your mum and dad have split up. Usually, your schoolwork tends to go down the toilet when there're problems at home, but you've done the opposite."

I couldn't look at him, and I did the old 'bite the inside of the cheek' trick to keep from losing it.

"My parents split up when I was about your age. It

was horrible. Before that, though, there'd been fights all the time. I couldn't wait to get to school to get away from home for a few hours. The first time I got into trouble at school for not doing my homework, though—something that never used to worry me at all—I knew I couldn't stand to have hassle at school as well as at home. I had to have some place I could feel good. So I started working hard. School became a bit of a haven for me. Maybe that's what's happening for you too." He squeezed my shoulder. "Nothing like turning a negative into a positive."

"Thanks, sir. I guess that's what I've been doing. I just don't want to sit in my room after tea with nothing to do, so I read my school books."

"That's great, Luca, but maybe a bit of variety wouldn't go astray. Look, I've got a load of books here. Do you want to grab a few?"

"I've never really got into reading that much. I wouldn't know what's good or bad."

"How about I pick a couple I think you might like, and we see what you think?"

I nodded, and he strode over to the bookcase, frowning in concentration as he scanned the shelves. I wished I had long legs like that. It'd be great to be tall. I looked down at my legs—solid enough but short.

I looked again a bit closer. Hair was sprouting down by my shins! Why hadn't I noticed it before?

Mr Squires turned back to me with three books in his hands and dropped them on the desk beside us.

"This one's an oldie but a goody, *Tom Sawyer*, and here's a light one by Paul Jennings. You might get a laugh out of it. The last one is *Lockie Leonard*. A West Australian wrote that one. Give it a go."

I leant towards him and smelt his after-shave or deodorant or something. It smelt good—not like Dad but still a bit blokey without smelling like a change room. "See you tomorrow, sir," I waved.

"Luca." His voice was sharp. I stopped and looked at him. "Believe it or not, it eventually gets better. It seems to take forever, but it does get there. The worst is probably over."

Good old Mr Squires. Well, not old, but anyway. The books were great, and I liked them all. They started me reading—he was right about that—but as for the worst being over, man, it hadn't even started.

School, and life, went on just the same till at last Grade Seven was finished and Katy and I were ready for high school. My life had settled into what felt like a holding pattern, but apart from the times Ray Reid was there—which was about three nights a week—things were okay. The hair on my legs kept sprouting, and I was quite proud of it. It made my legs look bigger and more muscular. I'd never make a great runner—my legs were too short—but I was getting faster and ran a bit further every morning.

Katy had changed too. She looked older than I did, especially when she got dressed up and Mum let her put on some lipstick. She couldn't wait to get to high school.

"Just think, Luca, we're used to about40 kids in the whole school, and there are nearly 400 at Geraldton."

I have to say I was a bit excited too. It felt like a big step, as though I was actually starting to grow up. I was starting to think Mr Squires might have been right after all, but then something happened that pulled me right back down to earth again.

It was Gary's birthday, and I was at his place for the night along with the boys in our class. We were lying around on sleeping bags in his old shed, and we had pizzas and cool drinks and a stack of DVDs. We'd already watched two, but they were pretty stupid.

"Have you got *The Hunger Games*?" I asked.

"Nah," said Gary, squinting at me with his good eye. "Wish I did."

"I've got it," I said. "I'll nick home and grab it." I was

already halfway out the door. Katy wasn't home that night either—she'd gone over to stay at her friend's place—but Mum would be able to let me in. I jogged slower as I got close to home. *Bugger, she must be out.* There were no lights on anywhere, but Reid's car was in the drive. They must be there unless they'd gone out somewhere close—maybe to Mrs Brockman's.

I walked up the side of the house in the darkness and tried the back door. Yahoo! It wasn't locked, so I opened it, ducked into my room and grabbed the DVD.

As I was feeling my way out the back door again after I'd flicked off the light, I froze. Mum's laugh came high and clear from her room. A man's laugh, low and gruff, chimed in with hers. There was no light under the door. His laugh. Mum's room. Within a heartbeat, it was all clear. I wasn't stupid. I knew what was going on.

I moved as quietly as I could, and once I was safely outside, I leant against the back wall and slid down till I was sitting on the ground. My heart was hammering, my thoughts were whirling around and my stomach was churning.

As I calmed down, one part of my brain was telling me, *Well, what did you expect? Dad's gone, Ray Reid's here all the time, they go out every weekend, and they like each other—so what?* and while I knew this was all very sensible, that thought was soon pushed away by a rage of disgust that had no words at all.

I got to my feet and walked slowly to Gary's. Surprised, the boys swivelled their heads and looked at me as I came through the shed door.

"Jeez, Luca, where've you been? We thought you must have decided to stop home or you got into trouble with your mum or something."

"No, I just took ages to find the DVD. Let's watch it now."

They all chorused agreement, and I handed the disc to Gary. A few boys wriggled over, and I settled down amongst the chip wrappers, the empty cans and the smell of pizza to watch the movie. I don't think I saw any of it. I was too busy with my own sickening movie running through my head.

Ray Reid was still there when I got home in the late morning the next day. He was stretched out on the veranda in Dad's cane chair with his big, bare feet on a stool. Mum was near him, and they were drinking coffee as they read bits of the Sunday paper. Mum looked up as I came through the gate. "Good party, love?"

I nodded curtly and kept walking towards the door to go inside, but her voice stopped me.

"Luca, could you just come and sit here for a minute, please?"

I frowned, dropped my bag loudly on the step and sat down on the edge of the veranda. As I did, Katy came wandering around from the back yard, munching an apple. Mum turned.

"Katy. Good. Sit down for a sec."

Katy finished the apple, even the core, leaving just the woody bit at the top like I always did, flicked it into a bush, plonked down beside me and leant back on the veranda post.

"What's up, Mum?" she said, licking her fingers.

"Nothing's up," Mum said, glancing sideways across to Reid. "Well, nothing's wrong anyway. In fact, everything's great."

Could have fooled me, Mother dear, I felt like saying, but I sat there silently.

Looking all pink and smiley, Mum said, "Ray's asked me to marry him, and I've said yes."

There was a silence. No, that word doesn't explain what there was. I could hear a crow way off, doing his five-call cry. *Why is it nearly always five?* I thought, and I remember following this thought almost excitedly. Had I cracked some secret bird code of communication?

Katy pushed her foot slowly against mine. I flicked my eyes across at her, and she widened hers at me. She was as stunned as I was.

"What do you think?" Mum said, her voice urgent and breathy. We both turned to her, and Katy slid her foot away from me. Reid was looking at us both too (me mostly) with a crease of—anger? concern? smugness?—on his forehead.

"Aren't you still married to Dad?" I croaked.

Mum shifted in the chair and licked her lips. "The divorce came through last week. That's what we were both waiting for."

Waiting for. Like you wait for the Royal Show or your birthday or a holiday. Waiting to finally wipe off Dad. I got to my feet awkwardly. "Does that mean you'll be here all the time? You'll live here?"

"We'll live in Geraldton," said Reid. "That's where I work, and that's where high school is for you two. Plus," he said, reaching his hand across to Mum's knee, "that's where your mum wants to live too. There's nothing keeping us here."

Katy piped up. "I love Geraldton. Luca, we'll be able to go to the beach every day after school."

I turned to her, shocked at the traitor she had become. "This is our home, Katy," I said, hating the wobble in my voice. "All our friends are here. This is where we've always lived."

Mum broke in with a note of irritation in her voice. "All your friends will be going to school there, Luca. There's no high school here! You'll see them every day."

I looked down at my hands, surprised to see them trembling.

Katy got up. "Gee, are you going to have a big wedding?" She sounded excited. It made me sick.

Reid laughed and said, "That's up to your mum, but I don't think so. Just us and a few friends. My sister, of course, and a few people from work."

"Would you like to be my bridesmaid?" I heard Mum say.

Katy gasped. "Oh, Mum, that would be great!" She jumped up and hugged Mum, and then, in front of me, she kind of skipped across and hugged Reid! I saw his freckly arms go around Katy, and I knew it was done. Once we moved from here, it would be as though Dad and our old life had never existed.

Anger surged through me at Dad. *Why did you go so easily? Why didn't you sell the house and move us all away from that toad? Mum would have been fine.*

She just got unhappy that you were away all the time and you were so cranky and tired when you were here. I started imagining what it could have been like— the four of us, maybe in Geraldton. Dad could have gotten a job there, and everything would have been like before. We would have been our old four-wheeled machine again.

But even as the pictures formed in my mind, I could hear Katy and Mum laughing and Ray's voice chiming in, and I realised there was a new machine now. I just wasn't part of it.

CHAPTER THIRTEEN

I came home from school a few days later, and a 'For Sale' sign had been hammered onto the fence. I wondered whether Dad would get any money when the house was sold. I supposed he wouldn't, but then if he cared about the house, he wouldn't have walked out of it so easily.

Katy was sitting on the edge of the veranda, swinging her legs and soaking up the sun. She had both arms stretched behind her like props, and her face was turned up to the sun. She was smiling a little and singing some tuneless little song. She looked so relaxed and happy that she made me feel good just looking at her.

"Howdy," she grinned, her eyes still closed.

"How did you know it was me? It could have been a murderer or a dog."

"I could say I smelt you," she giggled, "but I just

know the way you walk. We're going to Geraldton tomorrow."

"What for?"

She opened her eyes and shot a look at me. "Mum and Ray have seen a house they like, and they want to show it to us to see what we think."

I laughed, a short, derisive blast of contempt. "Yeah, like they really give a crap what we care."

She pushed herself up till she was looking straight at me. Funny how much she was starting to look like Mum. "Give it a rest, Luca. It's gonna happen, and it'll be heaps better than here. We won't have to catch a bus every day, there's more to do in Geraldton, and we'll have a nicer house than this old dump."

"I like this house," I said, staring back at her just as hard as she was glaring at me. "It's our home."

"Well, not for much longer," she sniffed, sliding down off the veranda. "Besides, it was never Ray's house. It's natural that he wants to live in his own place with his own wife."

"Not his own wife!" I yelled as she turned away from me. "He didn't have 'his own wife'; he came and took Dad's."

She turned and looked at me but kept walking away. "Sing another song, Luca. That one's boring."

123

Furious, I ran at her retreating back and shoved her as hard as I could. She sprawled face down into the gravel and lay there. The only sound in that horrible silence was my harsh breathing, and then she pushed herself up, brushed off the bits of gravel sticking into her hands and legs, and turned to look at me. Her nose was bleeding, and blood was trickling from both knees. I couldn't move; I'd never done anything like that before to anyone, let alone to her. We stared at each other, and then I heard the wire door bang.

"Katy! What on earth…" It was Mum, standing there, drying her hands on a tea towel.

"It's nothing, Mum," Katy said. "I just stacked it."

Mum jumped down from the veranda and put her arms around Katy. "Come in, and I'll put something on your knees and face. Oh, Katy, look at those hands! "

They stood there, Mum's back to me, her T-shirt loose over her tight jeans, and Katy's eyes burning into mine over Mum's shoulder. I wanted to run and put my arms around her too, even around Mum, so that everything would be good again and we'd laugh and go inside and have something luscious to eat and that warm, happy feeling of belonging would come back. But of course, I didn't move, and Katy's eyes closed as Mum turned her towards the house and they both climbed up the steps slowly and disappeared through the door.

That night in bed, I could see that Katy's bed lamp was on. I thought that she must have been reading or on her laptop in bed. I lay there, willing myself to say the words, and then out they came.

"Sorry, Katy."

There was no answer. I thought she must have gone to sleep and left the light on, but a couple of minutes later, the room clicked into darkness. I lay there feeling cold. I was alone, and it was all my fault. I looked at the clouds scudding across the inky darkness. The moon shone clearly through my window, and I looked down at the white sheet covering me. I only seemed to make a small bump in the moonlight. I wished we were younger and Katy would come snuggling under the covers with me again as my other half. We made a fairly big bump together, but alone, I saw I was nothing.

If Katy had been caught in the middle, somewhere between understanding how I felt and at the same time understanding Mum, it was over. The lines were drawn. We talked again almost normally after a few days, but something was gone. The impossible had happened. Katy and I, once two sides of the same coin, were separate people.

*

We got into the back of Ray Reid's car the next day with him and Mum up the front like they were married already and drove to Geraldton. We went down the gravel road and then left past the Greenough flats, where the trees, bent almost to the ground by the strong sea winds, looked like women on a battlefield stretching towards the ground, looking at their dead, their shapes fluid and gaunt. We drove past them and past the farms scattered along the way till the houses started appearing near the road instead of set well back like the farms. The houses clustered thicker until we were in the town itself.

We drove through the main street, out past the memorial, and there, half-way up a hill, was a two-storey house with a 'For Sale' sign and a short, fat man in a suit standing out the front. Reid pulled into the drive, and we got out. I turned away from the house and saw that there was a clear view of the ocean curving away from both sides of the marina.

I trailed along behind as we went through the house,

with Katy and Mum ooh-ing and ah-ing at every turn. I had to grudgingly admit it was a nice place: there were four bedrooms and big windows at the front where you could see above the roof across to the ocean, which stretched away to the horizon, the sun glittering off the crest of each ripple. I sat down on the front step and gazed at that view and then got up and sat in the car. No matter how nice it was, I didn't want anything from him, although I imagined the money from the sale of our house—the house Dad had bought—would come at least part of the way to covering the cost of this one. Katy came bursting out of the front door, and Mum and Reid stood talking to the fat agent.

"Isn't it amazing, Luca?" Katy called out to me. "We've got our own bedrooms with a bathroom just for us in-between. I love it!" She ran in circles on the lawn like a little kid. I turned away in disgust. Well, he's bought her, that's for sure—and from the smile on Mum's face, the deal's done.

We packed up to move six weeks later. It was frightening how small the pile of packing boxes was from our home when we left. With the shed empty of Dad's stuff, there was really only our clothes and a bit of kitchen stuff.

"We're going to have all new stuff," Reid said one

night after tea. "New lounges, new tables, chairs, beds, everything—for a new life." Katy and Mum sat snuggled up on the lounge, going through a pile of those house and garden-type magazines, their voices murmuring with the turn of each page.

We started high school two weeks before we moved, so we had those weeks of riding the bus to school with our friends. We'd clamber on each morning and rattle off down the road, past the waist-high wheat and past the dried pasture land dotted with clusters of dirty-white sheep and brown and white cows, skirting the main part of town till the bus pulled up outside the school gates. We'd jump down the steps, keen to be moving. Gary and I stuck together, feeling conspicuous in our crisp new uniforms and longing for them to look rumpled and worn-in like the older kids seemed to be.

The first day, we were gathered together onto a grass quadrangle, and then in a long, tedious calling out of names, we were allocated to various classes according to how smart the teachers thought we were. My name was called out early, and I went into the top class. I glanced across at Katy, but her head was down. She was clearly going into a lower class.

Luckily, a few kids I knew were in my class, so we

grabbed desks near each other. Part of me longed for the familiarity of my old school, but the sense of strangeness here was overcome by the excitement of change. I had thought I'd feel grown up going to high school, but we were at the bottom of the food chain here. The other boys were big and loud, and a lot of the girls looked like women, gathered in squealing groups or walking quietly in pairs.

Within a week, though, I felt more comfortable. The moving from room to room and teacher to teacher took a bit of getting used to, but as I got to know my way around, I started enjoying it.

We moved soon after. The last thing I packed into the trailer was the tool chest Dad had left me. It was too heavy for me to lift alone, so I lay a cloth down on the shed floor and carefully put the heavier things on it. As I dragged the chest awkwardly towards the trailer, Reid came out into the backyard.

"Here, give that to me," he said.

"I'm okay," I mumbled. As I walked back to the shed to pick up the other tools, I realised he was behind me. I crouched down on the ground, wrapping the cloth around the tools to carry them out too.

"Just a minute, Luca. I want to talk to you."

I stood, Dad's long Philips screwdriver still in my

hand, and turned to face Ray. He'd never been in here as far as I knew, and I hated that he was leaning so casually on Dad's old bench.

"I've just about had enough of you. You'd better change your tune, or things are not going to be too good for you when we move. I don't have to put up with a bad-mannered little shit in my own home."

"I have to put up with you in mine," I answered as calmly as I could.

Ray took a step towards me, his fists clenched by his side and his face twisted in a sneer. "That precious father of yours should have given you a few clips around the ear to knock that attitude out of you."

"Don't you mention my father," I growled, starting to breathe hard. "I had no 'attitude', as you call it, with him." I was panting now. "And you shouldn't even mention him. You didn't know him, never met him. All you did was sneak in here like a mangy dog when his back was turned." I couldn't believe what I had said, but it felt so good saying it.

Ray stepped closer, and his hand shot out. I was slammed into the tin wall of the shed with a clang, and I fell to my knees. My head was spinning, but I stood up and faced him, the screwdriver turned towards him and my arm raised.

"Keep away from me!" I rasped. Hot tears of rage mixed with pain blurred my vision for a minute, but I brushed them quickly away. We stood there, facing each other, his fist still up and my screwdriver pointing right at his stomach. I saw the fury in his face, the redness spreading down his neck, and the seconds ticked on, our breathing loud but slowing in the cool dimness.

His fist dropped. "You just go on thinking he was such a saint. Where is he now? How much of a father was he just to take off and never see you or your sister again? How much do you think he cares about you if he doesn't even bother to pick up a phone and talk to you, let alone actually come and see you?"

There was no answer. What could I say? The pain of hearing those words actually said out loud was worse than the throbbing in my face and neck.

"He just slid out of here like a mangy dog," Ray said slowly, a nasty little grin on his face. "Who's really the dog, eh?"

I lunged blindly at him, my hand tight on the screwdriver. He leapt to one side and shoved me hard. I fell awkwardly, and then I felt his big body crushing me under him, one hand pushing the side of my face into the rough floor of the shed, the other

131

one holding my wrist. The iron taste of blood was in my mouth, but the greatest pain was in my hand. He'd bent my fingers back till I could hold on no longer, and the screwdriver slid to the ground. He flicked the screwdriver away and twisted my arm up behind my back, his hot breath blasting me as he shoved his face down to my ear.

"Listen, you little prick, I'm here to stay. I've got your mother, I've got your sister and unfortunately, I've got you. But it's not me who doesn't belong here; it's you. The rest of us get on just fine. You're the only rotten apple in this particular barrel. All I can say is hurry up and grow up and then piss off. You're not wanted here. We're happier when you're not around." The weight suddenly lifted from my body as he stood up. I pushed myself up painfully but kept my face blank. I slowly brushed away the dirt that had been ground into the side of my face, clenching my teeth and glaring at his sweating, smug face.

"So, sonny, get a few things clear. I pay the bills. Remember that. You're just a snotty little kid who I can't stomach and who came with the package. Keep out of my way. Stay out as much as you like. You can sleep under my roof and eat at my table, but as soon as you finish Year Ten, piss off and don't come back. Go off and try to find your loser father, live under a bridge in Perth—I don't give a damn. I'll put up with you till then, but I tell you one thing." He paused, stepping closer to me, pushing that face I loathed so much right into mine, and to my horror, I'd involuntarily flinched away.

He laughed and then went on. "You raise a hand to me again, and I'll break your neck." He turned away then, brushing the dirt from his trousers and tucking in his shirt. Bending to the ground, he scooped up the screwdriver from where it lay against the leg of the bench.

"I'll keep this one as a souvenir," Ray said, and without another word, he stepped out of the shed. I stood there, pain shooting through my hand, my head and my face, but the greatest pain was knowing how powerless I was. For one mad moment, the thought surged through my brain that I would run away, thumb a lift to Perth, find Dad somehow. But the little fantasy dissolved at that point. What if I couldn't find him? Or worse, what if I found him and also found that he didn't want me around anymore than Katy and Mum did.

I stayed for a long time in that shed, so many feelings coursing through me at once that I couldn't think clearly, and then a shadow flickered near the door and stopped. It was Mum, standing there, peering into the dimness. She never came in here.

"There you are, Luca! Hurry up! We're in the car, waiting to go."

I lurched across to the tools, bending down stiffly to finish wrapping them up. God, it seemed like hours ago since I'd started this. I picked up the bulky roll clumsily and put it in the trailer and then slid in beside Katy, who just kept reading her magazine.

"Right then," Reid said, his voice chirpy, "We're on our way." We pulled away from the house, and I willed myself not to look back.

CHAPTER FOURTEEN

Life has become almost, well... pleasant. I don't really know if that's the word, but instead of feeling I'm being tossed around in some wild storm at sea—getting battered, going under, wondering if it might just be better to give up and sink to the bottom—now it's like I'm floating on calm water. Nothing much really disturbs me like before. I don't have time to think about what's happened. I have an answer for every rotten thought that pops into my head: be too busy to think. The dark days and nights going over and over what I had done are gone. Every waking minute is taken up—no slack time, no time to brood, no time to feel.

Straight out of bed when I wake up, stretches, push-ups, sit-ups, lunges, breakfast, school, lunch, trades, gym, duties, clean-up, tea, hanging out with Aaron and Archie in the rec, lockdown at 7.30, showering, studying or reading till 10, falling into bed, and sleeping like a rock till it all starts again the next morning. I'm getting through the work so quickly that Mrs Shiels calls me aside and says, "You're moving so far ahead of the class that I think you would do better working towards doing your Tertiary Entrance Exam. I've mentioned it to Mr Khan, and he wants to talk it over with you. Would you like to see him now, or do you want to think it over?"

I'm a bit stunned, really. I know I'm way ahead of the other kids, but I'm pretty comfortable in this class. The idea of actually getting stuck into all the subjects at TEE-level is pretty mind-blowing. But then Archie's words in the gym that day echo through my mind: "You got something better to be doing, white boy?" Maybe this is something to divert my mind even more. The idea of those exams at the end of the year is scary; it's one thing to feel you're doing well in a small group, but it's different to actually putting yourself to the test against thousands of other kids who've been plugging away without interruptions like court and remand centre! What if I totally bomb? I shrug inwardly. So what? Who'd know or care? Only me.

"Thanks, Mrs Sheils, but how can I be a class of one?"

"Mr Khan will sort that out," Mrs Shiels says, smiling.

She opens the door and speaks to the guard. The boys in the class are sitting in groups of four, their desks turned in towards one another, reading a play. Some voices stumble, but no one seems to be getting impatient. The group nearest me has suddenly gone quiet, and then a chorus of voices starts up. "Ben, it's your turn! You're supposed to be Victor! Keep up, ya knob!" but they all laugh good-naturedly, including Ben.

The only one in the class who isn't doing anything is Brown. He sits slumped in his seat, arms folded across his heavy gut, his face set and brooding. What's going on inside that mind of his? As the thought crosses my mind, he glances up from under that heavy brow and our eyes lock. His lip starts to curl in its customary sneer and then stops. Our gaze holds, and I see a strange expression cross his face. What is it? It's almost like he is in awful pain, and then Mrs Shiels calls me. The guard nods, and I walk up to Mr Khan's office alone and tap on the door.

"Come in." The door clicks behind me as I step inside, and Mr Khan motions to the chair opposite his desk. His hands are folded on the desk, his nails clipped, his skin smooth and brown.

Looking him squarely in the face, I say, "Mrs Shiels said you wanted to see me." I want to take control here for some reason; I feel the need to be something other than another waster passing through.

Mr Khan smiles slightly and then says, "She is very impressed with you. Based on what I've heard about you, so am I." He looks down, his hands rolling a heavy gold pen backwards and forwards. The clock on the wall behind his desk ticks slowly, and then he shifts a little in his chair, leans back and puts the pen to one side.

"The only problem I can see is that you have chosen not to take up the option of speaking to a counsellor. It is actually not an option; it's a requirement for all the boys here. The reason I haven't forced the issue with you is because I know you refused to say a word to the court-appointed one while you were on remand. I anticipated you would do the same here, and I haven't staff at my disposal to waste on anyone. Are you ready to speak to one now?"

I lean back in my chair as he had done and fold my arms. "There's no point. There is no deep, dark secret in my past. I know what I've done, why I did it and that I've got to pay for it."

He nods thoughtfully, his eyes hooded. "That's a very heavy burden to carry around alone. Talking to someone about it helps many people."

I shake my head, irritated. "Can anyone take the fact—or burden, as you call it—off me that I have killed two people, one of them my own mother?" There is no answer, and we sit there, those hideous words hanging in the air between us.

After a while, Mr Khan sighs and says quietly, "As you like, Luca, but that wasn't the only reason I wanted to speak to you. I really wanted to congratulate you on your effort in class. Mrs Shiels believes you have the capacity to sit your exams at the end of the year. If you would like to do that, there are several things I can to do to make that happen. Firstly, you may not be aware of it, but there are four boys here doing their TEE this year. They are all older than you, between 17 and 23."

"Twenty-three!" I burst in. "That's not a juvenile!"

"That's true, but there are some boys who are able to stay on here after they are 18 and serve out their sentences here rather than go to an adult facility."

"But where are they?"

"They live within the grounds here in a special self-care cottage where they look after themselves, and they're there because they have shown they have a strong desire to be rehabilitated. You don't see them much because they cook for themselves and they tend to be focused on their education, such as

139

getting accepted into an apprenticeship course or university when they leave here as well as general life skills. Mind you," Mr Khan adds, leaning forward, "every one of them has worked with his counsellor to understand the reasons for the behaviour that got him in here in the first place. The development that has occurred, both social and psychological, in each of them has convinced everyone concerned that they are determined to improve their lives and not get stuck in the revolving door syndrome."

I frown a little, and he continues. "The revolving door syndrome is where boys keep coming back in here, time after time. The worst thing is once they're 18, it's prison, and many of them end up spending most of their lives there. The thing is, Luca, they don't only cause misery for themselves but they spread it like a disease wherever they go. That's why it's so important to nip things in the bud here, and being able to talk with a trained person to understand what you've done is such a key part of getting past it and not slipping back into repeating the offence, whatever it's been.

"But look, today you're here for us to find a way you can have the best opportunity to get an education here. I suggest, if you are truly keen to put in the work, that you go across to the cottage to join the boys doing their TEE. I've already asked them if they're agreeable to that, and they are. So what I think is best is each day you can go there instead of Mrs Shiel's class. You'll come back here for lunch, and then instead of doing trades in the afternoon, you can go back and continue or study on your own."

He must see my face fall a little. I love trades.

"Perhaps you can join the trades class once a week if you can cope with the work. That's up to you. There's a teacher who comes in for a few hours each day to help, but the courses you'll do are mostly online, so you'll work to some degree on your own. How does that sound?"

"It sounds great," I mumble. Inside, I'm feeling a bit nervous. What if I can't keep up? What if, after all this trouble people had gone through for me, I fail?

"Apart from that, everything else will be the same. You'll still come back here in the afternoon, you'll still have your duties and so on."

"Is this all conditional on me seeing a psych?"

Mr Khan laughs shortly. "No, but I would like you to tell me the reason you're so against it. You're clearly an intelligent boy."

There is a knock on the door, and a worker from the

kitchen brings in a cup of tea and a couple of biscuits on a small tray. "Thanks, George." Mr Khan and the worker chat for a moment, and it gives me a bit of time to think. One part of my mind is saying, *Keep your mouth shut and say nothing. It's none of his business,* and the other part is saying, *He's gone out of his way for you; you owe him something.*

After the door closes and Mr Khan finishes a biscuit and sips his tea a few times, he puts down his cup and waits.

"Well," I start haltingly, "the truth is that there are a few reasons why I don't want to see a counsellor or case worker or whatever. Firstly, I'm not going to be a repeat offender." I glance at him and add drily, "After all, I'm not going to kill my mother and step-father again, am I?"

"No, of course not," he concedes, "but the fact that you were so out of control that you killed two people could indicate that this is the way you will deal with things in the future. Something upsets you, so you lash out and people get hurt."

I shift uncomfortably in my chair. "That's reasonable, but the thing is that I was never really violent before. It's not like I spent my time pulling wings off flies or getting into fights at school or even bullying anyone." I pause, the old familiar panic coursing through my body. "And then there's the fact that I was high. It's no excuse," I add quickly, "but you could say I wasn't completely in charge of myself." I am silent for a while. "You probably hear this all the time, but I know that whatever happens to me in the future, drugs won't be part of it."

He nods approvingly. "I believe you."

"Another reason—one I mentioned to you before—is that nothing anyone can say, no matter what a hot-shot psych they are, can change what's happened. No one can undo it, and there's nothing that can be said that will make me feel any different. It's like my friend from primary school who lost an eye. He's got a false eye, and it looks a lot better than a gaping hole, but it doesn't change the fact that it's fake and he's still as blind as ever. No matter what's said or what excuses are cooked up, the fact remains that two people are dead, it's my fault, and it's never going to go away." I'm panting slightly after all this talk, but there is still one more thing I have to say. "There's the last reason, the most important one as well: there's another person involved."

"What do you mean?" Mr Khan shoots back. "Someone else was involved in the deaths?" He leans forward in his seat.

"No, not like you mean. It's just that if I told the

entire story of what happened that night, someone else would get hurt badly."

"I don't understand. If someone else can explain what led up to the attack, don't you realise it could shorten your sentence? The judge only stipulated an indefinite term because you were so unresponsive and you seemed to show no remorse, no explanation for your actions."

"It doesn't matter," I cut in. "It's more important that nothing is said, now or ever. It can only cause more harm, and believe me, it doesn't change anything. I still killed them both."

Mr Khan slumps back in his chair and looks down his long, fleshy nose at me. "You're a strange boy, Luca. I can only imagine you did what you did in retaliation over something, a payback of some sort."

I feel my face harden. "Don't try to work this out, Mr Khan. I'm not a jigsaw puzzle you need to fit together."

He rubs his hand across his forehead, massaging above his eyes. "You're quite right. Let's get back to what I can help you with. You'll need to sit down and go through the subjects you can take." A wry smile lights up his face. "If you do well in the exams, you'll still have another year here before you turn 18. You could begin a university course online."

"I don't think that far ahead," I say wryly. "There was no date set for my release, so as far as I'm concerned, I can't make plans for a future that may not happen. My future is probably adult prison. I'm not living a fantasy here. I just want to get through my time, whatever it ends up being, one day at a time."

We sit there for a while, saying nothing, but it isn't an uncomfortable feeling. I can see a photo on the side of the desk. Mr Khan is standing next to a tall, slightly stooped guy of about 23 or 24, who is dressed in the cape and mortar board—I think they call it—of someone who just graduated. A small, round woman wrapped in a red and gold sari, her smooth black hair pulled back from her face, stands on the other side of him, one plump arm encircled with rows of gold bracelets resting lightly on the young man's—her son's—arm. Something convulses through my body, and I want to be out of there, now.

"Shall I get back to class now, sir?"

Mr Khan starts slightly. "Yes, of course. On Monday, you can meet with your teacher, and he can discuss your options with you and set up a schedule of study." He stands up and reaches across the desk, his hand outstretched. "You've done well so far. Keep it up."

I take his warm, dry hand and shake it firmly, the

way Dad taught me. He opens the door for me, and I leave. The siren goes as I walk back down the corridor. I wait for all the boys to file out and then catch Mrs Shiels' eye.

"All sorted?" she calls, bustling around the room, picking up papers and books.

"Yes. Thanks for your help." I would like to say more, but the guard motions for me to go for lunch, and the opportunity is lost.

CHAPTER FIFTEEN

There are other things to think about besides school. I'm getting better at football, and even though I sit on the bench a fair bit of the time, when Mr Robinson gives me the nod and I'm out there, it feels pretty damned good. I've put on a bit of weight, and now when someone runs into me on the field or I'm caught up in the pack, I don't get flattened the way I used to. Archie had been right. All that running comes in handy. I don't have the best kick in the world, but I can run and keep running. A lot of the guys don't do much exercise apart from the Saturday games; I'm in the gym with Archie every day.

The Saturday after I'd spoken to Mr Khan, Mr Robinson calls us over at the end of the game and we plonk down on the grass, glad to be resting. He stands there, his ruddy face serious as he raises a hand. There's silence, and then he grins.

"Good news, boys. The Kwinana under-18s are coming here for a match in two weeks. Think we've got a chance?"

"They any good?" Aaron drawls lazily, his long, golden body sprawling on the grass.

"Not too bad at all. They've beaten some good Fremantle teams this season."

Archie nudges me and murmurs, "That means they're pretty good. Nearly all of the best league players come out of Fremantle."

Some of the places I hear of down in Perth are just words to me, but I remember Fremantle. Dad had relatives down there, and we'd stayed with them for a week on holiday once. I'd only been about five or six, but lots of that time was stuck in my brain. We'd gone out in someone's fishing boat, had fish and chips on the beach and wandered around the place a lot. It was full of little shops and laneways and cafés. Dad said it was much better than Perth itself because it had a European flavour. I didn't really know what that meant. I thought it meant the food was different. The streets were full of people having coffee, sitting in the sunshine and just having a good time, it seemed to me.

There were lots of Italians, and I remember how happy Dad had been talking with his friends and family. It had felt funny to see that he belonged to someone other than us, but those people were so friendly. I'd never been hugged and kissed or chucked around and swung up on shoulders so much. If ever I get out of here, I'll go there again.

I turn back to Mr Robinson's voice. "So, boys, the only way we'll beat them is to go out there and play as a team. I know you tend to rely on Archie." He pauses as kids reach across and pat Archie's back and laugh at his obvious embarrassment, and then he goes on, "but we can't go out there as a one-man wonder. We're a team, and everyone has a part to play.

"Now this Kwinana team will have strategies they use every week so that every player knows exactly what to do. No random kicks hoping they'll lob somewhere in the right direction, but planned moves. Good footballers use their brains, not just their bodies. I'm going to be here every afternoon for the next two weeks, and Mr Khan has given permission for you boys to train instead of going to afternoon lockdown after trades."

We whoop with joy. Every day! Outside, running around instead of stuck in our cells. I wonder how they'd managed to get enough staff to be on during all those training afternoons. Maybe they want us to win the game as much as we do.

149

We all jog back to the gym, and a couple of guards are jogging with us. There is a new guy I haven't seen before. He's bigger than most of the other guards— not taller, but it's easy to see that he works out. His head is shaved, and I can't see his eyes because he's wearing sunglasses, but his jaw juts out, square and aggro-looking.

Archie flicks a look at him too. "Steroids."

"How do you know?"

"Look at that jaw. I dunno; they just get a look." The guard turns as we watch him, and he pushes aside a couple of boys at the back of the pack, moving through to where Aaron is. He stops and says something to Aaron, his big beefy hand resting on Aaron's back.

Archie frowns. "Bit too friendly." We push through into the gym and lose sight of Aaron, and in the rush of showers and changing, I forget all about the guard.

Everyone is pretty pumped up that day, full of talk about the game coming up. We cluster in the rec room, and the guards wander past, checking us out casually through the observation windows every now and then. I catch a glimpse of that guard again, just standing there, looking at us.

"Think I'll give the gym a miss today," says Archie. "I'm stuffed."

"Same here." I'm fine, but I feel like company. Dangerous. "Arch," I say, before my brain can stop my mouth, "where you from?"

Archie glances at me from those deep-set eyes. "Up around Carnarvon way."

"What's it like there? I've never been further north than Northampton."

Archie stretches out in a corner on an old beanbag and closes his eyes. "Beautiful. Black-fella country. The dirt's red, the sky's always blue, it's always warm, but there's plenty of rain when you need it. Not too many buildings."

"Your family still up there?" I hold my breath after I speak. Shit, what if he asks me about mine?

"Yeah. Most of 'em. Some have drifted down to Perth, but I've got plenty of cousins, aunties and uncles up around there. Much better place to live than down in Perth." He pauses and chews on his thumbnail for a minute.

"So you've got brothers and sisters?" Better to get this away from parents. His face brightens, and he nods vigorously.

"Eight of 'em!"

"Bloody hell!" I laugh.

"I'm an uncle already. My sister Charlene has two

little boys, and my oldest brother, Raymond, has a daughter. He lives up in Broome. I wouldn't mind going up there one day."

"Nine kids is a lot of work for one woman."

"Yeah, I guess so. I think Mum wanted to have a big family to make up for what happened to her mum."

"What do you mean?" I ask.

"They never talk about it, but my cousin Bella told me that our grandmother Rosie was a half-caste. That's what they used to call Aboriginal people who had one white parent. It was easy to see, even when she was old. Her skin was a kind of patchy light brown, and her eyes were... what's that colour called that's not brown, not green, not blue?"

"Hazel."

"That's it."

"Who was her father?"

"Christ knows. Some white prick." He flashes a quick look at me, grinning a little apologetically. "Sorry."

"Don't be. A prick's a prick whatever colour he comes in."

Archie nods. "Back then, they took what they liked. The thing is it ended up being a curse for her."

"What, the people in her family didn't like it that she had white blood?"

"No, that wasn't it. She was just a kid, and her mum had other kids; no one made any difference at all between them. Her stepfather loved her, and she was the oldest, so she helped her mum with the others. When she was about seven or eight, some government people visited the camp and looked at all the kids. No one took much notice. They thought it must be some sort of health check, but the government people picked up four kids and put them in the back of the truck. Rosie was one of them.

"'It was awful,' Bella told me. 'They were all screaming, and Rosie's stepfather ran over and grabbed one of the men. The others knocked him to the ground and kicked him. All the women ran after the truck as it left. Rosie's mum got her hand through the rails of the truck, but she fell as it sped up. The last she saw of her mum she was kneeling in the road, blood running down her face.'"

"Jesus," I say, quietly. "Why'd they kidnap them?"

"They'd taken all the kids who looked a bit white. It's what they did then. They'd take them away from their families, give them a white name and put them in schools run by the church. God knows what my grandmother's real name was."

"What happened to her then?"

"Well, she had to stay in there with other girls until she was 14. She learned to read and write a bit but mostly how to clean and cook. Bella said that my grandmother hated the nuns, but she grew to love Jesus even though she couldn't work out why He was so kind but these women, who said they were doing His work, were so mean. Anyway, she used to ask every new kid who came there if they knew her family, but no one ever did.

"When she got to 14, she was handed over to a family on a station. The wife treated her all right, and my grandmother cleaned the house and looked after the kids. The husband was away a lot, fencing. Anyway, to cut a long story short, he started coming to the little shed she slept in. She was too scared to say anything to the wife. It was too shameful to her, but it wasn't long before the woman noticed her belly getting bigger. She'd screamed at her and called her a slut, and a day or two later, the man had driven her back to the convent.

"They took her back, but no one spoke to her except to say she was a sinner. All she could think of was that as soon as the baby was born, she'd just leave and the two of them would keep walking till she got back home. She made little clothes for it, but as soon as it was born—and I say 'it' because the nurse threw a cloth over her face so she couldn't see whether it was a girl or boy—they took it away. As much as my grandmother cried and pleaded with them, she never saw her baby, that day or ever."

Archie shakes his head slowly. "Bastards. As soon as my grandmother was strong enough, she climbed out a window and just kept walking. She knew to go north, and eventually she landed in Carnarvon. She wandered around, looking for her people, but they were all gone. The town had spread, and there was a banana plantation where the camp used to be. Somebody told her that her mother had died.

"She never found any of her family again. There were different mobs further inland, and she lived with one of them and eventually had Mum and four other kids. Bella said she still cried over her first one, though, right up until she died.

"Mum's done her best with us, but it hasn't been easy. I just want to get out of here, go home and look after her proper. Maybe get a job around home or go up North for a while and make some money." Archie stops talking for a while, and then he turns to me, his eyes very dark. "I've gotta get out of here, Luca. It's driving me mad. I know I haven't got long to go, but being inside like this is killing me. I'm used to sleeping outside. Even though Mum's got an old house on the edge of Carnarvon, we nearly all sleep outside. I feel like I can't breathe properly when I'm stuck in that cell. I just need to keep my nose clean, keep away from trouble, keep my head down. One thing wrong, and I won't get out. One of my cousins kept coming in here and getting into trouble with the guards, and he ended up going to big prison when he turned 18. He couldn't stand it either."

"Is he out now?"

He laughs bitterly. "You could say that. He hanged himself the second week he got there."

We sit there for a while. What can I say after that?

"What are you two knobs looking so sad for?" It's Aaron, bouncing around from side to side in front of us. He looks hyped up, a big grin on his face, bobbing around like a boxer.

"We're sad 'cause you're here, dickhead," Archie laughs.

"No you're not. You won't be sad in a minute, anyway." Aaron glances at me, his eyes grave for a moment. "Something to tell you, Arch," he says quietly, his hand across his mouth, pretending to wipe it.

I get up. "Think I'll go and see if the canteen's still open."

Archie's hand shoots out and grips my arm. "You don't have to go." He turns to Aaron. "He's okay. You can talk in front of him."

Aaron nods and shrugs slightly apologetically. "Just keep your mouth shut, Luca."

They both laugh, and I look at them, puzzled. Archie punches my shoulder lightly. "You hardly ever open it! You're the quietest dude in here."

"Anyway," Aaron goes on, "that new guard has been talking to me a bit, and he says he can get some sweet stuff for me, bring it in."

Archie shakes his head. "Don't tell me about no drugs. I don't want to know."

"What about you, Luca? You must have a fair bit stashed in your account. You never seem to buy much like the other guys. How about something to make the time pass?"

I close my eyes for a moment. No thoughts, just longing—yearning—surges through my brain, and then I crush it, snapping my eyes open. "Not my thing. Thanks anyway."

"Yeah right," Aaron smirks. "I saw that look on your face. You want it bad."

"Maybe, but I'll never touch it again." My voice shakes a little.

Archie grabs Aaron's arm. "Leave it alone. Why's that guard hanging around you?"

Aaron shrugs. "Just being friendly."

"Bullshit. He's after something, and he's setting a nice little bait for you. You watch him. Keep away from him. He's a bloody faggot."

Aaron snorts. "Don't be stupid. He's built like a tank."

"Do you think they all wear frilly dresses?"

Aaron screws his face up. "You're on the wrong track. He's an okay guy."

Archie turns and spits in the corner. "For a smart guy, you sure can be dumb sometimes."

Aaron shrugs. "More for me." He opens his mouth to say something and then closes it again. "Catch you." Then he bounces away, boxing lightly into the air.

Archie shakes his head. "I can't stand drugs. Makes you do crazy things. Them and grog."

"What drugs have you done, Arch?"

"I haven't. It was drink that got me in here—drink and being dumb." He shakes his head, a look of pain crossing his face, and lowers his voice. "I've probably done something a lot worse than anyone else in here." His voice catches in his throat, and he turns away, coughing unconvincingly. "I've killed two people,

Luca," he says at last, head down, not meeting my eyes. I don't breathe. "Most of them are in here for theft or malicious damage, some for assault or even rape, but not too many are in here for causing someone's death." I can see his long eyelashes beaded with tears in the harsh light. I wish he'd stop, but he goes on.

"We kids used to run pretty wild. We nicked off from school a lot or just didn't go at all for weeks, so we had plenty of spare time. When we were younger, it was easy. We were happy just hanging around, maybe swimming or fishing, but when we hit about eleven, we wanted to do more. A few kids sniffed glue, but they just sat around like zombies. There was an older kid, Ryan, and he knew how to break into cars, but I'd never done anything like that.

"When we could though, we'd get older kids to buy beer for us, and we'd drink it even though it tasted like shit at first. We wanted to look tough, like men." He shoots a quick look at me. "You know how it is. Anyway," he goes on, sighing deeply, "one night we went to a party at Ryan's aunty's place. We snuck heaps of wine and beer without being noticed. We walked into Carnarvon, up the main street, making a racket and kicking bins over. Ryan was jogging from car to car, testing every door, and then we heard him whistle in the darkness. We saw the inside light of a four-wheel drive go on. Someone had forgotten to lock it.

"We crammed into the back seat and next to Ryan, who was under the dash, hotwiring the car. He was a genius at that. Within about 30 seconds, the car started, and we were off down the road. We kept the lights off and drove slowly down the street, did a U-turn at the end near the fascine, and then we were off. Ryan drove pretty fast, and we were all yelling, and then he pulled over, opened the door and spewed."

"'You drive for a while,' he said to me. 'I feel bad.' I was so excited. I'd never driven before, but I knew where everything was and this car was automatic. I slid over, and Ryan got in the other side. I pressed the accelerator, and we crunched back onto the road.

"'Give it the gun, Archie!' the kids in the back screamed, so I pushed my foot down on that pedal hard, and we jerked forward and roared down the road. It was easy. The road was straight and long, and we just laughed ourselves stupid, the window open, the wind whipping through the car.

"I started feeling a bit sick myself with all that grog sloshing around in my gut, but I didn't care. I could do anything. Then Ryan shouted above the noise, 'Slow down!' I ignored him and put my foot down harder, and all the boys cheered. He tried again. 'Slow down! The turn off to Perth's up ahead!' I jammed my foot on the brakes to slow down, and the car just slid and jerked and rolled. I thought it would never stop. That car just went on and on, sliding and people screaming and…" Archie's panting now, and his top lip is dotted with sweat. I put my hand out and touch his arm, but he doesn't seem to know I'm even there.

"I came to in the darkness, the car lights still on and beaming ahead, but inside the car, there was nothing but someone crying in the back. I tried to speak, but something was stopping me, and it took a long time for any sound to come out. When I could finally speak, I whispered as loudly as I could, 'Jimmy, Ryan, Brett…' right through all their names, but only one answered apart from the one who said nothing, just kept crying like a puppy whining. I don't know how much later the ambulance arrived, and then there were lights and noise and voices everywhere.

"I woke up in hospital. My shoulder and arm were in plaster, but I was okay apart from a bad headache. I asked the nurse how everyone was, and she said the doctor would speak to me. The doctor came in a few minutes later and sat down. I remember his face really well. It was long and sad-looking, and I could see he hadn't shaved and most of his face had that blue look. I still see it."

Archie stops, and I see his chest rising and falling fast as he catches his breath. "The doctor said, 'Well, you're okay. In fact, you can go home tomorrow. You've had a bad bump on your head, but the breaks in your arm are clean. Your friends didn't do so well. The one called Ryan broke his neck and died at the scene, and another boy died 10 minutes ago. Apart from that, there are concussions, the odd broken bone and internal injuries.' Then he'd said the words that will stick with me forever: 'Was it worth the ride?'

"I'd sat there in the bed, saying nothing, his words hammering into me, but I was really only hearing two of them properly just then: 'Ryan...died.' I kind of stopped thinking then. I was in some kind of a daze, like my body was working but I was somewhere else."

Archie lets his head flop back on the headrest of his chair and closes his eyes.

"Me too, Arch," I say quietly.

He opens his eyes and looks at me. "What do you mean?"

I swallow. "Two people are dead because of me too."

His eyes widen, and he grips my arm. I feel my bottom lip start trembling out of control, and he blinks fast too. We sit there for a minute, and then he shakes his head, wipes his eyes quickly with the back of his hand and smiles.

"Look at us sitting here like a couple of snivelling old tarts. I've never talked so much in my whole life." We both laugh uncontrollably, and Aaron comes over and says, "What's the joke?" We find this incredibly funny for some reason, and we're still laughing, tears of—what?—running down our faces, when the siren rings for us to go back to our cells.

CHAPTER SIXTEEN

Katy fit right into high school. She loved everything about it, and by Year Nine, there were plenty of boys hanging around her. She was popular and good at sport, especially softball. Life for her seemed perfect.

I liked it too. I'd started to grow but not as fast as most of the other boys. I'd always remembered Mr Squires' words about making sure you didn't have any hassles at home *and* at school, so I didn't make too much of a pain of myself in class and I did my homework because it was better than being around Reid, plus I wanted to prove him wrong. I wasn't a loser.

One weekend, Katy knocked on my door and said, "Luca, I've got a game at Dongara tomorrow. Mum said we could stay there tonight at the hotel and come home tomorrow afternoon after the game. Do you want to come?"

"Is he going too?"

She sighed and pursed her lips, the bright lip gloss she wore making her mouth look like a squashed tomato. "Of course he is; duh!"

"I'll pass, thanks."

"Okay, I'll ask Erin to come, then." Katy shrugged and left, her face blank.

Mum came in a couple of minutes later, a frown on her face. "Come on Luca, you'll enjoy it, and you'll be on your own overnight if you stay here."

"I'm 15, Mum! Just go! I don't want to, and Katy will have a better time with her friend than with me."

Mum screwed up her mouth, just like Katy had. "That's not the point! We're going as a family!" I couldn't keep the look off my face, and she turned away angrily. "Do what you want then!"

Half an hour later, they left. Mum stuck her head in my room before they went and said, "There's cold meat and salad in the fridge and plenty of bread for breakfast and sandwiches tomorrow. I don't want anyone here while we're away, so no inviting any friends over. We'll be back by tea time tomorrow night."

I looked up from the book I was reading and nodded, and then she was gone. As soon as I heard the car drive off, I put my book down, leant back on the pillow and stretched. The joy of it! The whole house to myself! My room seemed to expand around me. It was nothing like the little old room I used to share with Katy. This one wasn't super big, but it had everything anyone could want. There was a big built-in wardrobe with mirrored doors, a set of deep shelves for all my books, and a chest of drawers.

The best thing was the window. It was wide and filled the room with light. There were plants outside to hide the neighbour's fence, but the right side of the window was clear of them, and I could see sky and sea across the tops of the houses lower down. I even had a glimpse of the war memorial, a white dome of metal gulls that glinted in the sun and glowed under a full moon. I had put my study desk under that window, which sometimes served as an escape hatch late at night. I'd only done it a few times, but it was easy to slide it open early on so that no one would hear me go out later. Originally, I'd just gone for a walk around the silent streets on a hot summer's night when I couldn't sleep, but lately I'd been joining a few kids down on the beach.

We'd just lie around and smoke a bit of dope. It was easy to get at school. Kids came into school from farms, and lots of them had stashes of marijuana they'd grown in some hidden place. It was easy to grow and dry, and they'd pack it into little cellophane bags and sell it pretty cheap. We'd stretch out on the sand, the waves rolling in and out and the moon washing everything white, and we'd puff away.

The big black dome of sky above us was that same one Dad and I had lain under, but how much more beautiful it was when I was high! No longer was it a scattering of stars. Now each one, as I looked at it, seemed to pulse forward and stand proud of all the others. I could have reached out and touched them. Each perfect star filled my vision, and everything else faded away around it. All I needed to do was look a little to the left or the right, and a new star—as though waiting just for me, for my undivided attention— would merge with my brain, its light filling my eyes, my mind, and soaking down through every part of me.

I had felt so relaxed. Everything was perfect. I loved my friends, the breeze, the sand under me, the sound of the waves. I wished I could stay there, held in the arms of each moment forever, but then it would slowly wear off and I would be left lying on the sand, getting cold, with the stars once again way beyond my reach. The other guys around me would start stirring, and we'd drift home, our mouths dry, our movements dream-like.

Well, tonight, I'd be down on the beach again. Someone would be there. I had a job at a café on the beach, and it was enough to keep me in weed. I didn't smoke it a lot—just down there, really. I'd never have brought it into the house. Someone would have smelled it, and Reid would have said nothing while Mum went off at me, but in his eyes, I would have seen his glee at my turning into the loser he'd predicted I'd be.

My glance dropped down to my desk. All my books were lined up neatly, the way I liked them. Mum had put a photo there of Katy and me taken at our primary graduation two and a half years before. I picked it up. Katy had changed. She was taller, and her hair was long and shiny instead of in those dinky little ponytails she'd worn back then—and me, well… I looked closely. I looked so young in the photo. Then I crossed the room to my wardrobe and looked hard at myself in the mirror.

I was pleased with what I saw. I hadn't exactly grown a lot in height, but I was heavier, and my arms and legs were lightly muscled. I didn't look like a kid, that's for sure. My face had squared off around the jaw a bit. My eyes were dark and intense, and my nose didn't look so long anymore. My face had kind of grown around it. *I'm not bad looking!* I thought with a grin. My skin was olive, like Dad's, and there was a look in my eyes that hadn't been there back in primary school—kind of wary, as though I were sizing people up. In the photo, my eyes were kind of open and soft, like a child's.

I'm becoming a man! I thought proudly, and I turned side-on, stuck out my chest and struck an 'Arnie' pose. Then I had to laugh and shake my head; there was still a fair way to go. I was still a skinny 15-year-old kid.

I had a bit of homework to do but not today. This day was mine, and tomorrow too! I made a sandwich, put some music on and turned up the volume, singing along as loudly as I wanted. This was great! I left the stuff on the bench—I could clean up later—grabbed some money, my bathers and a towel, and I headed out the front door. This is what it was going to be like every day when I grew up and left. I'd have my own place and I could do exactly what I wanted.

It was a hot day, and by the time I'd jogged down the hill to the beach, I was sweating. The harbor stretched to the left along the far arc of the water, concrete silos like fat, grey test tubes huddled next to the wharf. To my right lay the marina, a few squat fishing boats rubbing shoulders with the odd yacht and pleasure boat. I pulled off my shoes and crossed the street to the beach, waving to a few kids I knew who were kicking a footy along the beach. I ducked into the change rooms, peeled off my sticky clothes and pulled on my board shorts.

Within three minutes, I was in the water, diving under the waves that were rolling over lazily a few metres out. Lying on my back, I kicked out until I was past them, and then I floated for a while, my eyes closed, body rocking rhythmically as the swell surged beneath me.

Something slid close by me, and I jerked up. There were plenty of sharks around Geraldton, so I struck out for the beach, willing my pounding heart to quiet down and not send distress signals through the water. Then I heard a high burst of laughter. Karol, the Croatian girl who'd started school here a few months before, was treading water in front of me. Every boy in my year lusted after her. She was tall and athletic but slim, with green eyes and the smoothest skin I'd ever seen. And that skin, lightly tanned and gleaming wetly, was right there banded only by two tiny red strips.

"You think I'm shark?" she laughed, smoothing her wet hair back from her forehead.

"You can eat me any time," I grinned back and then ducked under the water in embarrassment. *What a stupid thing to say! She'll think I'm just a sleazebag now,* I thought, but when I came back up, she was smiling just the same. Thank God her English wasn't good.

"Can you show me how to do that riding of the waves without a surfboard?"

"Body surfing?"

"Yes, yes, that's right," Karol said.

"No worries. We need to come in a bit closer to the shore."

We swam in towards the beach a little to where the waves started swelling. Karol couldn't swim very well, but she loved trying to catch the waves. Bad luck she was always too slow and didn't really get a decent ride.

After she'd tried about a dozen times, I said, "Here, get behind me and hang on tight around my neck, and I'll show you what to do." She grabbed me round the neck. "Aaargh!" I choked. "Too tight! Don't strangle me!"

She laughed, a real laugh, and I joined in. God, she was gorgeous, the salt water droplets caught in her eyelashes, her teeth white, her skin honey. Then

I felt that smooth skin pressed against my back, and she hooked her arms under mine and held onto my shoulders.

"Not strangle now!" she said. I could feel every bump and curve as she clung to me. Thank God the water was cold. I could have just stood there forever and died happy, but she said impatiently, "When do we surf our bodies?" I snapped my head back and saw a nice little wave starting to gather strength.

"As soon as I start swimming, just kick as fast as you can, and if we time it right, the wave will carry us with it. Now!" I lunged forward with her clinging like a barnacle. We rode it right to the beach, and then she let go and we both rolled in the sandy water, trying not to gulp in any of it as we gasped with laughter. Her bikini bottom had ridden up, and the white skin looked so silky and touchable, and then she hooked them back into place with a shy laugh.

"Ha! I have sand in places where sand should not be!" she said, wading back out to where it was deeper, and I could see she was sluicing water through those straining red strips of cloth.

"I'll do it, I'll do it," I breathed silently, and then she struck out towards the deeper water, calling over her shoulder, "Again, Luca; I want to do it again!"

And that's how the whole afternoon went. If only it could have gone on forever. Finally, she said through chattering teeth, "I must become warm again. Look at my hands!" I looked and saw they were white with a bluey tinge. I grabbed one of them and started to drag her towards the shore. My God! My boardies were baggy but not enough to hide the mini-tent happening at the front. *Shit! If I run up the beach with her, one of my mates will notice and burst out laughing. Everyone will see! Karol will be disgusted!* Quick, horrific visions of lying on the sand and looking like a ski jump or tripping and pole-vaulting on the beach ran cartoon-like through my mind. I let go of her hand and said, "My towel's just near that flag. Lie down on it, and you'll warm up in a couple of minutes."

"Are you not coming?" she asked.

"I just want to catch one more wave, and then I'll be there." I turned before she could think of anything else to say and swam out fast. Five minutes later, I was nearly back to normal and ran up the beach and flopped onto the hot sand. It was so delicious, the contrast of hot and cold, those funny shivers coursing through my body.

She lay on her back, her arms folded over her face. I was belly down for safety, with my head turned towards her, resting on my elbows. I closed my eyes, but through my lashes, I was running my eyes from her toes right up to her raised arms. She was so close to me, her thigh touching mine. I lay my head down on my arms and just wallowed in the warmth of that long, smooth leg pressing lightly against me. *Hell, here we go again!* I wriggled into the sand, and then suddenly she sat up and began pulling her T-shirt over her head. "Thank you so much, Luca! I like that very much. Could you teach me again another time? I must go home now."

"But why? We could have a hamburger on the beach later. There are always people here Saturday night."

Karol shook her head decisively. "No, my parents would not permit that. I must be home before dinner."

"Why not come down here after that?" I persisted.

She laughed, twisting her long, dark blonde hair back into a loose bun on top of her head. "I am not allowed out at night alone with a boy for another two years, but I can see you at school and here at the beach on the weekend." She smiled and then bent down and touched my cheek. "Thank you very much for today. You are very kind." Then she turned and walked quickly across the sand. When she reached the road, she turned and waved—how did she know

I'd be watching her?—brushed the sand off her feet and was gone.

My mind was buzzing. How your life can change in a couple of hours! Before, she'd just been another pretty, out-of-reach girl in an ugly school uniform; now she was a golden goddess, warm and beautiful, and she liked me! She was going to come to the beach again. I lay back down on the sand and started imagining what might happen the next time; us swimming and then my arms around her underwater—maybe later, under a towel, a big one. I would have to buy one. This one was too small.

My mind drifted on.

"What're you doing, Luca? Want to get a burger?"

I sat up quickly. Three guys from school were there: Ross, Brian and Toby.

"Or do you want to lie there having a wet dream over that Croatian chick?" They laughed like drains, slapping Brian, the joker, on the back.

"Yeah, right, very funny." How right he was! Then I jumped up and ran at him, knocking him into the sand, and we rolled and scrambled, laughing, until we hit the water.

Watching the sun drop towards the horizon and the sky changing colour, eating a burger, pretty much in love, no one at home—life couldn't be better. For some reason, Dad popped into my mind, but I pushed him out again as quickly as I could.

CHAPTER SEVENTEEN

When it got dark, we went for a walk through the main street. I have to say, there was a lot more to do and see in Geraldton than where I'd come from. I still missed it, but I missed it like I missed being in primary school or playing hidey or helping Dad in the shed. It was time to put it away in my mind. All over.

We met a few other kids and hung around across the road from the pub in a small park. The music was really pumping out of there, but the bright lights, noise and people laughing just made us feel a bit depressed, I guess. It seemed like forever till we would be able to walk in there, order a beer, lean on the bar and talk, and then get into our cars with some good-looking girl and drive to wherever we wanted and do whatever we wanted.

"This is boring," said one of the girls, Ebony. She wasn't bad-looking—great, in fact, from the neck down—but she had such a snooty look on her face that it turned you off.

"Well, what do you want to do?" said Ross. Things were different when girls were around. Everyone acted like tossers and said dumb things, crude things, bragged about themselves—anything to get attention.

"I feel like going to a party, don't you, Amanda?" Ebony's friend was nicer than her but shy. She nodded eagerly, and they both turned expectantly to Ross.

"I don't know about any parties anywhere, but why don't we get someone to buy us a few bottles, and we'll go down the beach and see what pops ups." The girls squealed with laughter, "Let's go!" and ran off, doing that weird run girls do when they're wearing tight skirts and high heels—kind of like their knees are hinged to kick out sideways instead of backwards.

Ross muttered, "You guys go ahead. I'll try and get some booze." The others pulled out a few notes between them and handed them to him.

"I'll stay with you," I said quickly as everyone else took off after the girls.

"Got any money?"

"Sure. I got paid yesterday."

"Don't spend it all on beer." He stepped towards me and lowered his voice even though the racket from the hotel was drowning out anything anyone else might hear. "Toby's got a stash."

"Great. I like it better than beer anyway." We stood for a few minutes, scanning the people flowing in and out of the doors to the bar, and then Ross saw someone he knew. He jogged forward and grabbed a tall, skinny guy in a checked shirt and black jeans by the arm. They talked for a few seconds, and then Ross handed him something from his back pocket—maybe cash, maybe weed. Anyway, the tall guy disappeared down the side street to the bottle shop at the back and then walked across to the darkness of the park with a slab of beer. He went behind the toilet block, and when he came back out, he was minus the slab. We walked casually over to the toilet block, and Ross picked up the beer up and tucked it under his arm.

Five minutes later, we were sitting between sand dunes not far from the water and giving out the cans of beer. We lit a small fire and sat in a circle around it, silent apart from the giggling girls who seemed to spill more of their beer than they drank. I didn't like the taste much, so I stayed with the one can while the rest of the boys kept on drinking. The silence didn't last for long as the alcohol started working, and before long, Ross and Brian had moved in on the girls.

A few minutes later, they got up to 'go for a walk', and the rest of us sat there, laughing and messing around but with envy clear on everyone's face. Not mine, though. I had the thought of Karol to keep me happy.

When the talk lulled, I touched Toby's arm. "Got some?"

"Yep," he said, reaching into his jacket and pulling out a packet of weed and some papers. I handed him the money, and he took it and turned back to the other boys. I rolled the paper carefully around the dry weed and licked the edge to stick it down. I smiled to myself when I remembered the time Toby had thought he could charge us more by doing all the rolling beforehand and selling them ready-made, but we'd all said, "Yuck! We don't want to smoke your spit," so he sadly went back to selling his little packs. The fire died right down to a dull glow, mirrored in miniature by the pinpoints of light in the darkness where each of us lay smoking. I threw my towel over me and drifted off.

Later—who knows when—Toby loomed beside me and sat down. "Want something a bit stronger?"

"Like what?"

"I haven't got any here, but I got some speed from a kid at school."

"Where'd he get it?"

"Who knows? Who cares? Do you want to try it?"

I considered his offer. I had no intention of becoming a druggie, so I didn't take anything but the occasional puff, but hey, this was different. I felt so powerful, so adult, that day. Why not try something new to mark my new life? Soon I would have my own gorgeous girlfriend, and it would be so good to be close to someone again.

"How much?"

"I haven't got much, so maybe just $20 will do it."

We lay there for a while, the sound of the waves lulling me to sleep, but it was getting cold and I was so thirsty. "I'm going. I've got work tomorrow." I said.

"Do you want to come over tomorrow and I'll give it to you?"

"Sure. I knock off at 2.30." I looked at the dark bumps lying on the sand. "Ross and Brian didn't make it back?"

"Nah. Probably took those two slags home. Think I'll go too."

We walked up the beach, our mouths dry and heads hazy, and waved to each other. I was home 20 minutes later and asleep not long after that.

*

I had an early shift the next day, and the coffee shop was pretty busy. A bus load of tourists kept me flat out bringing their coffee and cakes, cleaning the tables and working on the till. Near the end of my shift, I heard the low purr of a powerful car pull up outside, and I glanced out quickly. A tall blond guy I hadn't seen before got out. *Lucky,* I thought as I cleaned a table of crumbs, ripped open sugar packs and spilled coffee.

As I juggled the cups and plates back behind the counter to the kitchen, I heard, "Hi, Luca." There she was—Karol! She was with another girl I'd seen at school. "You know Luca, don't you, Michelle?"

"Yeah, of course. You're in my science class."

Karol smiled at me, that beautiful, open smile that I felt was just for me. "We're here with Michelle's brother and his friend." I turned and looked, and there, laughing with his friend and leaning back in his chair in the window, was the blond guy with the car. "Can we have four coffees please? Two cappuccinos and two short black?"

I nodded, took the money from Michelle and gave the order to the barista.

"Bye!" They turned and walked across to the table. As Karol squeezed around it, the blond guy turned and pulled the chair out for her. She sat down and leaned towards him, her hand on his shoulder.

"Get a move on, Luca. There are two orders here waiting." My boss stood there, frowning.

"Sorry," I murmured, grabbed the first tray and whisked it over to Table 17. Then I took the second one outside, where people were sitting under the umbrellas dotting the stretch of paving between the shop and where the sand started. By the time I got back to the counter, the order for Karol's table was ready. My hands were shaking slightly, but I took a deep breath and carried the tray over. I put it down on the empty table beside them and handed out the four cups. Not a drop spilled.

"Thanks, Adam," smiled Karol, touching the guy's arm again. "This is Luca, a friend from school. He is teaching me how to surf the waves without a board."

He flicked a dismissive glance at me. "So how's that going, babe? Getting the hang of it?"

"I think so," she said, smiling up at him, her eyes all sparkly and wide. Picking up the tray, I carried it back and forced myself not to look across their way again. I collected the cups from outside and wiped down the tables, and then a few minutes later, I saw them get up and walk out, holding hands. The four of them walked along the beach, and then I saw Adam put his arm around Karol's shoulders and she snuggled up to him, her arm going around his waist.

I went outside and wiped the tables again mechanically, my eyes unable to pull themselves away from Karol. It was so painful that my chest hurt, and for one horrible moment, I felt tears prickle my eyes before I blinked them down. Pushing my way back through the café doors, through a crowd of chattering Japanese tourists, and I circled methodically around the tables, cleaning, smiling and taking orders like a demented robot until Jerry, my boss, called me over.

"That's it for the day. See you next week."

I changed back into my clothes and then caught a glimpse of myself in the mirror. Who was I kidding? What chance did I have against a good-looking 18-year-old with a car? Walking outside into the glaring heat, I stood undecided. I felt like going home and rolling up in a ball, but chilling out with Toby seemed a better choice.

Turning left, I trudged to Toby's house. I could hear the music booming out from his room at the back, so I walked around the side and banged on the back door. The music stopped, the door swung open and he was there, grinning at me. "Thought it might be you."

I followed him to his room, and we sprawled onto a couple of old chairs. He bent down and pulled out an envelope taped to the underneath of the chair he was sitting on. I flicked two $10 bills at him, and he handed me a tablet and took one for himself. "I can make this up for you instead." From the bottom of the envelope, he fished out a small, plastic syringe.

"Nah, just a tablet. I don't want to start shooting up. This is just a one-off, and then the odd bit of weed is enough for me. I don't want to end up with a fried brain."

He snorted but dropped it back in the envelope. "Whatever. You'll feel different after you've had one of these. Take another one for later."

"I haven't got any more money on me." It wasn't true, but I didn't want it.

"No worries. You can pay me at school tomorrow." He was being a bit aggressive, which wasn't like him, so I guessed he must have taken something already. I took the tablet and put it in my pocket. I'd give it back to him tomorrow. I didn't go to work to spend my money on drugs. I'd saved up nearly $2,000 from my work. I'd need it when I left home.

"Take one now, and then we can head off. Maybe go around to Ross's. My mum'll be home soon, and she

185

can always tell if I've had something. Don't take the other one today. You don't know how you're going to react the first time."

I was regretting it a bit now. I didn't want to stagger home and have Reid know I was off my face. His words had never left me—that I'd end up under a bridge in Perth. I'd just take this tablet, hang around Ross's till it wore off, and then go home. I'd buy a pizza and hang out in my room tonight. I gulped it down while Toby was taping the envelope carefully back under the chair, and we came around the side of the house just as Toby's mum pulled into the drive.

"Hi, Mrs Williams, "I said, waving at her as Toby hurried past the car, his head down. "We're just going for a walk."

"Okay, Luca," she smiled. Her old station wagon was full of kids and dogs and boxes of fruit. "Be back for tea, Toby!"

"Sure, Mum," he called back, pulling his cap down over his eyes. I caught up to him, and we jogged up the road. The sun was still high, but it had lost some of its kick.

"Feeling any different?" Toby's eyes were bloodshot under his gingery eyelashes.

"Mustn't've worked," I shrugged.

He laughed. "Just give it a bit more time."

Ross's house was a few blocks away. His parents were wealthy, and there was a long, semicircular drive leading up to the front door. I remember there was a big garden, but what was in it I had no idea until today; as we turned into the drive, the colours of the flowers and the trees seemed to pop in my face. Hibiscus, frangipani, palm trees—I hadn't realised there were so many greens! I stopped and picked a fallen flower from the ground. Its petals arched away from the centre, the stamens stretching towards me like tiny arms. The colours! There was red, but that word wasn't enough; it was luscious, velvety, deepening like rich, strong blood as it flowed into its throat. I had never seen anything so beautiful.

Toby sniggered. "It's kicking in, man. Enjoy the ride." I turned my head to speak, but the movement of the trees above and around me—so gentle, so different to each other—made me forget what it was I had been about to say. He grabbed my arm. "Let's go around the back way."

"No," I managed to breathe, my voice so loud, my breathing fast. "I want to walk. No, I want to run!" and I turned right onto the footpath without a glance back, the stones crunching beneath me. It was as though I'd been looking at the world through a light haze, and it had suddenly lifted, and I could see everything—sharp, unique, new. Energy raced through my veins, and I had to run.

Down the road, skirting the main street, waiting so long when a car came; darting between cars, too impatient to wait and knowing they couldn't hurt me, and then the sand, the beach, the waves. I bent and pulled off my shoes and threw them over the little wall behind the café, and then I was off, the sand light and warm under my feet. I ran like never before, loping smoothly with no effort. Every wave surged at me, diamonds of water hurtling at my approach. I was a king, a master of the earth! My body would not tire! I would run like this forever, past the straggling beachgoers and past the boats snuggled together at the marina until there was only me, the sand, the sky and the vast stretch of ocean.

From far away, I could hear my breath rasping, but my pace never slowed. Gulls scattered from my path, screeching and wheeling, and I felt that with just a little more effort, I could have leapt into the sky and soared and banked into the wind with them.

At last, I slowed and flung myself down on the sand. The sun had dipped low, and I lay there marvelling at whatever had created that vast sprawl of colour and light, every cloud edged in gold, nestling plumply and softly in the heavens, waiting for night.

I must have dozed for a while, and when I woke, it was getting cold and the wind had whipped up the sand, blasting it against my bare legs. I got to my feet and turned back. The sky had darkened, and the first few stars were out. The desire to run had gone, and I was covered in sweat, my head thumping dully.

I trudged back the way I had come, the feeling of power ebbing now, and in its place, the memory of Karol and her friends. The more I thought, the angrier I became. That guy was just like Reid, sneaking in under my guard. Some part of me knew this wasn't right. I had no claim on Karol, and I certainly wasn't her boyfriend in anyone's eyes but mine—but that didn't stop me. If I had run into him then, I know I would have smashed him. I didn't care how old he was or how much bigger, I would have flattened him.

My head was really pounding, and my mouth was dry. By the time I got back to the café and put on my shoes, it was dark and the streets were pretty much deserted. Not much happened in town on a Sunday night.

I put my hand in my pocket to buy a drink, and

I felt the little plastic packet and pulled it out. The tablet glowed dully in the dimness. I raised my hand to throw it away. To take it home, perhaps to be found by Reid, was too dangerous; I had contained my pot smoking to when I was out with friends for the same reason. But then some little kid could pick it up and think it was a lolly. *What the hell. How bad could it be?*

I opened the edges of the little bag and swallowed the tablet. I still felt angry because of Karol. I thought that maybe it would make me forget all that and take this bloody headache away at the same time. I leant back on the wall of the café and watched the stars. The sky was black, and the sea breeze had whipped up the surface of the water and made the masts of the yachts hum and make that strange ticking noise they always did in the wind. The moon rose higher, and still I sat.

Things were so perfect on the outside and so stuffed up inside. I felt so alone out there on the beach—Dad gone, Mum not the same person, and Katy, once my other half, had become a distant acquaintance, like an old friend you waved to at school but didn't care enough about to talk to. And now Karol. I had to laugh a bit wryly at that. What a tosser I was! As though she would be interested in me! Everything I loved left me.

It was time to go. I got to my feet and walked back

through the dark streets. The flicker of a television was visible through the odd window, but mostly everything was dark. It must have been later than I thought. I felt strange. My head was still aching, and instead of feeling amazed by everything around me like I had been feeling earlier, I just felt like a ghost sliding through the streets alone.

CHAPTER EIGHTEEN

No lights were on as I walked up the drive. Reid's car was in the carport though, so I figured they were all asleep. I stopped uncertainly with the key in my hand. I just didn't want to wake anyone up and start a long conversation. "Where were you? Why are you out so late? I told you we'd be home by tea time," and so on and on and on. I just wanted to get inside and into my bed and to sleep, and maybe this dull rage I felt somewhere deep down would be gone in the morning.

Just then, a car sped past the house, and I twisted the key, its noise covered by that of the car. I pulled off my shoes and closed the door as quietly and slowly as I could. Tiptoeing down the passage, I passed the lounge and the dining room noiselessly. I was nearly there! I just had to get past Katy's door and then the bathroom, and my room was next. I knew my way pretty well in the dark, but I forced myself not to rush and kick something over.

I stopped. Katy's door was open. I could see it in the soft moonlight through her window. She never slept with it open, and I could see her inside, crying softly, sniffing and drawing in shaky breaths. I opened my mouth to whisper to her, and then I heard Reid's voice, low and soothing. Frozen, my mouth still open, I remembered hearing him once before from inside a bedroom—Mum and Dad's bedroom in our old place.

I staggered, stepped forward and switched on the light. Reid was sitting on the side of Katy's bed, dressed just in his pyjama pants. His round body, covered in ginger hair, turned, surprised, one of his hands outstretched towards me and the other on Katy's shoulder. Katy was sitting in bed, blinking in the harsh light, her face red and swollen. The moment seemed to stretch. Once again, I could see details so clearly—the pulse jumping in Reid's throat, the bitten-down nails on his hand, the tree outside rasping lightly at the window—and then rage, hot and powerful, surged through my body.

I lunged at Reid, my outstretched hands aiming for his throat. He jerked sideways and fell to the floor but was up again in a second, and his fist caught me hard on the ear. I hit the dressing table, and it crashed backwards, the corner catching my leg. I was dizzy with pain, but it felt a long way off. I felt powerful again, unstoppable. I pulled myself up, half-tripping over something rolling under my foot—Katy's baseball bat. Scrambling to my feet, I clasped the end of the bat in both hands and braced myself against the wall.

Reid stared at me, his eyes bulging, and as I raised the bat, he lurched towards me, face contorted and hands raised. A mist covered my eyes, a red film. *So you really do see red!* I had time to think, time to act! Not like that time so long ago in Dad's shed. As he came at me, I stepped to one side and swung with all my strength. Ah, the sweetness of that moment! Years of anger—at Dad, at Mum, even at Karol and that guy today—all surged together to focus on the start of it all: Reid!

The bat smashed into Reid's temple, and he stumbled towards me. God, he'll kill me now! I swung again, wildly, again and again. I could hear screaming, but I had to keep going. Something pulled at my arm, but I shook it off. There was someone else there in the haze between me and Reid.

"Out! Out of the way!" I tried to shout, but only a roar came out as I kept hitting and hitting till I sank, gasping, onto the floor.

I lay there, my head, my heart and my blood pounding. My breathing slowed gradually, and I felt the carpet pricking my face, my jaw and head aching, my shoulders and arms throbbing and a soft, strange moaning in my ears. I opened my eyes and looked at Katy. That sound was coming from her, huddled on the bed, her arms wrapped around her knees, staring into space, rocking and mumbling to herself.

"Katy!" I whispered. She didn't look up. I rolled painfully on my side, and my foot touched something. *Christ! Christ!* I pushed myself up onto my hands, my eyes staring but my mind not working.

Reid's leg was sprawled next to me, and he lay on his back, the side of his head a pulpy mess. Thick, dark blood oozed across the bridge of his nose where brighter blood congealed. Mum was lying across him, her face on his shoulder, turned away from me.

I've killed him, I thought. *He's not just unconscious, he's dead!* His eyes were open, staring up at the ceiling. *Oh, Mum! What have I done? I hated him, but you loved him.* She lay quietly, not even crying, with her arm so protectively across his chest. There was nothing I could say to her. I got to my feet groggily and sat down.

He had to be stopped. Dad wasn't here to protect

Katy like he should have been, but I was. I put my arm around Katy's shaking shoulders. "It's over, Katy. He can't hurt you."

She stopped shaking, stopped breathing even, and turned to face me. Her eyes were huge, filled with tears, looking at me as though she didn't know who I was, and then her hands flew up, and she raked her nails down both sides of her face, screaming at me unintelligibly.

Shocked, I jerked back and slid from the edge of the bed onto the floor, staring at her. Then I turned away and looked straight into the dead, white face of my mother.

*

I can't really remember what happened after that. At some point, I was somehow in the passage, dialling Emergency and speaking calmly to someone on the other end, but it wasn't really me; it just looked like me.

I was huddled somewhere a long way away.

CHAPTER NINETEEN

My new course starts next week. I'm going to do English, Mathematics, Human Biology, Physics, Chemistry and History. Mrs Shiels says it's a good, broad course that will get me into plenty of university courses if I do well enough. I don't really think about that side of it. One day at a time. Just today. The future is a foreign land.

Monday arrives, and Owen walks me across the yard and across neat squares of concrete to the cottage, and he knocks at the door. The cottage looks so neat, almost like something you'd see in a fairy tale—the cottage in the middle of the woods. There are some vegetables growing in beds on either side of the door. The only thing ruining the picture is the barbed wire on top of the perimeter fences and on the roof.

A stocky boy opens the door wide. "Hi, sir," he says,

studiously not looking at me. He has the long, droopy face of a basset hound.

"G'day, Bruce. Boys," Owen says as we step inside. Closed doors face onto a central room, a combined lounge, kitchen, dining room and study. "This is Luca. He's the one who'll be working in here every day." A couple of boys nod, their faces impassive; the rest don't react at all. There is a silence that goes on too long, and then a boy, taller than the rest, steps forward.

"Hi, Luca. I'm Damien, and this is Norbert, Jamie, Jason and Bruce."

The boys nod but make no eye contact.

"Well, I'll be back at 12.30," Owen says and leaves. As soon as the door closes, a couple of the boys go back to the kitchen, but the others sit at the computers that are spaced around the perimeter of the room. One of the doors opens, and I see a neat bedroom with posters on the wall, and another boy comes out. Damien takes pity on me again and calls from across the room, "Mr P will be here in a minute. He'll sort you out. Just grab a seat." I go and sit at the table, trying not to feel too much like a complete tool, and look at each boy.

Jason is Asian, short and slim, with black-rimmed glasses. He's sitting nearest me, and I can see he's working on some sort of maths program with equations clustered across the page. He's tapping rhythmically, and I turn to a boy slumped in his chair. He looks as though he's half asleep, but his fingers are flying over the keys, his head turning slightly from side to side as he takes notes from the screen. Norbert. Right. Norbert's blond and has a tat written in that old Gothic printing on one of his forearms. I crane my neck a little to read it. *Wir sind das Volk*. Whatever that means.

Someone drops a cup in the kitchen, and the boys all stop and laugh. "You dopey dickhead, Jamie!" Bruce, the one who opened the door, says, but I can't remember any more names. Easy to remember his name—Bruce the basset hound. They're cleaning the kitchen, sweeping the floor and stacking dishes into a cupboard.

It's a pretty neat setup for a bunch of boys. There are bars across the windows, but they are the only things that really remind you that this is prison. There is a television, lounge chairs and a table with cards laid out on it—very cosy, but it makes me feel like an intruder. After all, I'm younger than any of the boys here, and I have the privilege of being in their cottage without really earning that right.

There's a scraping of feet on the mat, and then the door swings open.

"G'day, Mr P."

"Hi, sir; how's it hangin'?"

"Very well; thanks, boys. I can see you're hard at work already." Mr P drops a couple of folders onto the bench and ambles over to the first computer—Jason's— sticking his hands in his pockets and leaning forward eagerly. While they talk about the work, I turn and scrutinise him.

He's a strange-looking guy. His shoes look like they're from the 80s—slip-ons, scuffed and split here and there. God, does he have odd socks on? It sure isn't meant as a fashion statement judging by the rest of him. No, one is just inside-out, so they look different. His trousers are too short for his long legs, they are made of that shiny stuff you don't have to iron and they're pulled up too high around his gut. His shirt is light blue—no ironing needed as well— and there is a button missing, so I can see a singlet! Who wears a singlet unless they're 100? His collar is crumpled, and I can see elastic underneath it, which his tie hooks into. Whoever this guy is, he doesn't give a crap about how he looks.

He moves from boy to boy, his voice low but warm,

encouraging. He points to a maths problem Norbert must be stuck on and laughs out loud, slapping his leg. "That's why it's wrong, you silly bugger!" and Norbert laughs back, shaking his head ruefully. Each time he finishes with one boy, that face that had eyed me off so hostilely is grinning with pleasure before the boy gets back to work.

I wonder if he is deliberately avoiding me as he comes to the last boy and then steps across to the window, arms folded, legs wide, rocking slightly forward and back, his head sunk deep in thought. He isn't tall, but there is something dynamic about him that I can't fathom given the random way he dresses.

Then he turns, and his eyes fall on me. They're blue and piercing and deeply set into his craggy face. His nose is large and slightly hooked, and his mouth is a thin, firm line, but it's the eyes that hold me. There is an intensity in them—as though he's sizing me up, gathering me in—a thick crease forming across his nose as he focuses. A smile crosses his odd face, and it morphs into a delighted grin, his eyes softening. He leans forward as though in a rush to get to me, as though his legs are too slow.

"Ah, sorry, mate. I've forgotten your name. Bloody hopeless with names. Wish I could just call everyone

201

'mate' all the time, and then I wouldn't have to worry."

His smile is infectious, and I smile back.

"Luca, sir."

"Course it is. Interesting name. Italian, isn't it?"

I nod.

"Good workers, the Italians. Look at all those roads they built through England when they conquered it. All straight, solid buggers, still there. And the way they build their houses! Built to last. Love their concrete." He stands, musing for a moment. "Righto! Well, my name's Karl Pietrowski. I'm Polish—well, my parents were. I was born here, and whenever I said I was Australian, my father would say…" Here all the boys interrupt him and chorus raggedly, "So if you were born in a stable, would that make you a horse? You've got Polish blood on both sides, a Polish name, a Polish face. You just happen to be lucky enough to live in this beautiful country."

They all laugh as they finish, and he says, "Yes, well, they've heard me say that a few times before. Just call me Mr P." I nod. "So, you want to do your TEE. Think you can do it?"

I shrug uncertainly. "I hope so. I'd like to have a go at it."

"That's the way!" He slaps me hard on the shoulder.

"So let's get started." He shows me what I'll be expected to cover in maths for the year. I can see there's a lot to do, but it isn't really daunting. Hell, I have the time. It isn't like I have anything else to do. He sets me up at a computer and starts me on the first chapter. Everything is pretty much online.

"If you get stuck, just sing out or else email me if I'm not here. I'm only here a few hours a day, so make the most of me."

I nod and start working my way through. It's tougher than I've been doing, and the time goes by quickly. I am deep in the questions that follow the first chapter when I feel a shove in my back. A cracked mug full of Milo slams on my desk. "Wash your cup when you've finished. You can make 'em tomorrow."

"Thanks," I croak at the receding back of the basset hound. I lean back, and the other boys swivel in their chairs to face each other, stretching their backs and slurping their Milo. Mr P stands there and throws his head back, and I watch his throat jerk as he swallows the whole mug in three gulps.

"Thanks, boys. See you tomorrow." He drops a folder on each desk. In my folder, there are notes on the next chapter and some questions with a scrawled note: To Do Tonight. I glance at the clock. Only an hour to go.

I still have a fair bit to do. A couple of boys wander around the rooms, munching on apples, but the rest are glued to their screens.

Half an hour later, I'm done. I glance through the questions Mr P has left me. They're pretty complicated but not too bad. I close the program down. How to kill the next 30 minutes? My brain's too fried to do the questions now, but I sit there with the notes in my hand, pretending to read them.

"Have you finished, kid?" It's Norbert. I swivel on my chair to face him.

"Yep. What about you?"

"Just about. I'll do a bit more later. Going to do your TEE, eh?" He speaks with an accent that I can't quite pin down—Dutch? Swedish? German?

"I hope so," I shrug. "They seem to think I can, so I'll give it a go."

"What do you want to be?"

The other boys are silent now, listening openly to our conversation.

"Not really sure. Maybe something medical." Don't know where that came from. "Hard to really imagine a future."

Norbert flicks a quick look at me. "Just have a plan for when you get out and stick to it."

"And don't do the same shit again that got you in here in the first place," the basset hound calls out. The others murmur in agreement. The hard look is off his face now, and I feel a pang of meanness for the name I've given him. Bruce. Bruce—that's his name.

"No, that won't be happening."

"Well, just work your arse off and keep your nose clean, and you'll be right," Bruce says, and the boys nod in agreement.

There's a light tap at the door, and Owen comes in. A knock at the door! These guys have it made. "Okay, sport, it's time to go."

I gather my things quickly, and as I step through the door, I turn. "Thanks for having me," I blurt out awkwardly, like some well-trained kid at a birthday party.

There's a mumble of "No worries," and "See ya tomorrow," and I'm outside in the fresh air, walking back across the quad. My head is heavy with all that maths, but I feel great. Life can be okay at times, even for me.

CHAPTER TWENTY

The major focus of my days now is the football game just under two weeks away. I've scraped into the team as a rover, and we have training every afternoon until the match, so I'm starting to feel pretty handy. I'm fast and can actually jump quite high, so as long as I don't get flattened by the bigger guys, I'm not too dusty. Nothing like Archie, of course, but I'm better than I was. Nothing can compare with pulling your boots on and getting out there in the fresh air. If you don't look at the high fencing everywhere, you can only kid yourself that you're free.

Aaron's in the team too. The only drag is Brown, but I can see now that he's not out to get me especially; he just hates everyone, and it makes him feel good to hurt someone. Mind you, he's pretty effective. He's slow, but while the other guys are fumbling around in a pack and fighting for the ball, he just wades in there like a bowling ball through a stack of pins, and nothing can stop him. Anyone a bit slow gets knocked down, and he just grabs the ball and boots it—not too straight, but man! So far!

Mr Robinson is working us hard and wants us like machines. No dithering around when we've got the ball, stick to the game plan, play fair. Every day's the same. We have 20 minutes of warm ups, and then he goes through marking, kicking goals, and defending until finally we play a short game. We're stuffed at the end of each day—legs wobbling, sweat everywhere—but it feels good.

"They're a solid team, boys, but so are you. No show ponies here; play as a team." Mr Robinson says. We roll our eyes behind his back. Archie's so much better than all of us, even if we are playing as a team. "No one person can go flat out for four quarters; nor can they be everywhere at once! Remember that!"

*

Saturday finally comes, wet and overcast with a fine drizzle, which we know will soak us and make holding a ball and keeping our balance pretty hard. No probs. We're really fired up to win. All the boys are egging us on, and I receive quick pats on the back and thumbs up from boys who'd never even looked at me, let alone talked to me, as we queue for breakfast.

I can't eat much, and Archie nods with approval. "Drink plenty of juice to keep you going but not too much food. You won't be able to run, and you'll spew if you cop one in the guts. Do the same at lunch."

Tim is jumping around, picking at his food too.

"What's the matter, squirt? What are you nervous about?" Aaron says.

Tim's good-natured little rat face creases in a grin. "I just want you to win. They'll be thinking they're so much better than us."

Aaron nods and looks at me. "He's right. They'll be trying to put us off our game. Take no notice of anything they say—'specially you, Arch. They'll be out to get you when they see how good you are."

Archie shrugs. "I've been called plenty of names plenty of times by white blokes. Don't worry me."

The siren rings, and we go back to our cells to do our jobs. I finish quickly and try to read to pass the time, but I find I've been looking at the same page for 20 minutes without taking anything in, so I just sit, picking at my nails. What if I play badly? What if the winning goal is down to me and I stuff up? I'm starting to feel sick, and then finally, it's lunch.

We eat quickly, the dining room a hum of excitement—which doesn't make me feel any better. At last, we're taken to the gym, and we sit cross-legged on the floor, Mr Robinson in his usual spot on the edge of the stage.

"Well, boys, this is it. The other team has arrived, and they're in the quad. As soon as all the boys are seated around the oval, we'll go out. I want you to go and do your best. No dirty play, Mr Brown," Mr Anderson says, shooting a quick look behind me. "Just remember: we've trained as a team, so go out and play like one. After the game, we've invited the guests to a sausage sizzle with us, and I know you'll have enough good manners, irrespective of the outcome of the game, to treat them all well." He pauses. "I'm proud of the way you've all worked." The door squeaks open, and a guard nods to him. "Right. Everyone's waiting for us. Let's go."

We spring to our feet, keen to get started, and as we jog outside onto the muddy ground, all the boys huddled under tarps strung along the fences cheer and clap. We feel like heroes running out there, the shouts and whistling making us all grin.

The other team is sitting on the benches, trying not to check us out too obviously. We run up to our bench, feeling like Roman soldiers coming into battle, and stop when Mr Robinson holds up his arm. "Welcome to our visiting team. Mr Moore will toss the coin."

None of us, including the other team, can stand still. We're all twitching and jumping up and down. We win the toss, choose our end and run to our positions. The umpire bounces the ball, Aaron leaps up and knocks the ball straight to Archie, and he's off. Within 15 seconds, we have our first goal! The kids watching on the sidelines go wild, screaming, whistling and punching the air. We caught them flat-footed!

We jog back to our spots, not one of us able to keep the grin off his face. I make sure I don't make eye contact with the guy I'm on, but I can see that his face, peppered with a smattering of angry-looking pimples, is sour. "Enjoy the goal, jailbird," he hisses through his teeth. "There won't be many more." I grit my teeth and keep my mouth closed.

But there are! We're buoyed up by that first goal, and by the end of the first half, we're six goals seven to their four goals two. We run off for the break, and Mr Robinson crouches in front of us as we sit sprawled and panting on the bench and on the grass.

"Right, boys, you're doing well, but now it's crunch time. You need to calm down and think more clearly. Those seven points are seven times you could have kicked goals. You're playing hard, but you're going to run out of steam if you don't start playing smart. Remember the plays we practised. Straight down the sides. Hand pass more carefully. Don't rush when you've taken a mark. Understand me?" We nod as we slurp water and rub our aching legs.

The siren sounds for the second half. "Aaron, Luca, Martin—take a break. I want you fresh for the last quarter." The reserves leap to their feet joyfully and jog off with the rest of the team. We flash dark looks at one another. We all feel the same; sitting on the bench when we want so desperately to be out there is torture, but Mr Robinson's the coach and that's that.

The other team's coach joins Mr Robinson at the edge of the oval as the teams get into position. The boy I've been on stops and speaks quickly to a few of his mates, and then they break and run off, grinning to one another. What the heck are they up to? It doesn't take long to find out. They're a bit older than us, and some of them look like men from where we're sitting. They get the ball after the first bounce and kick long and straight towards the goal. We hold our breaths as it soars straight on target, but then out of the pack, those long, brown legs of Archie's propel him up, right in the mouth of the goals, the ball landing sweetly in his hands just like it was aiming for them all the time. We roar with delight, our three voices joining those of the other boys. Good old Arch, always right where you need him.

As the teams jostle for position, the opposing team's goalie moves close behind Archie, and we see him punch Archie hard in the small of the back. Archie stumbles forward but doesn't lose the ball.

"Ump!" we shout, leaping to our feet, but both umpires have moved back with the rest of the players, waiting for Archie's kick, and they can't see what has happened. We sit there, powerless.

Archie's kick is beautiful, and the boys start playing like professionals, using the tactics Mr Robinson has taught us—but the other team are just as determined to stop us any way they can. Always with an eye to where the umpires are, they 'accidentally' crash into our boys, and from where we sit, we can see elbows and knees gouging under cover of the writhing boys. We scream ourselves hoarse, and the umpires split up a bit more, realising what is going on. Within a couple of minutes, two of the opposing team's players are sent off for foul play.

They are booed as they run back to their bench, and play goes on a bit cleaner, but as the minutes tick by and we score more goals, the game gets even rougher. It's Archie they're concentrating on now. There's a solid core of three of their team always on him, shoving him, running into him, bending close to him and spitting words as they run past. We see him shake his head as though flicking away flies, but he's exhausted and angry-looking by the end of that quarter.

Only a few points separate us as the siren sounds. Mr Robinson runs to meet the boys, signalling us over to joining them. We leap up, fresh and raring to do battle.

"I don't need to tell you how dirty they're playing," Mr Robinson says. "Archie, take a break for 10 minutes." We groan. "Don't worry, I'll put him back on. The refs know what's going on, but it's not easy to catch the offending players."

"It's not just that, sir," one of the boys pants. "They never stop with the comments, especially to Archie."

Mr Robinson snorts derisively. "You're not a bunch of girls. Let 'em go. It means they're rattled. Just keep on your man and don't let them put you off your game. Remember, you're out there to win, fairly and squarely."

The siren sounds, and we run to our spots. Last quarter. Got to beat these pricks.

"What ya in for? Raping a gran?" It's the idiot again. I open my mouth to say something and then snap it shut. That's what he wants. I take off to where the game is, and he's a breath behind me. Then I'm down— he tripped me as he ran past. "Sorry, mate!" he laughs, landing heavily on my outstretched hand with his boot, the sprigs gouging between my knuckles before he's off.

I scramble to my feet, pressing my hand hard into my leg and racing after him, and then I stop. I'm in the clear with no one near me. Archie spots me and boots the ball in my direction. I leap into the air and pluck the ball from the sky, the pain in my hand a strange counterpoint to the joy in my heart. Then I turn and kick the ball straight to Brown, who grins, his pointed teeth zigzagging familiarly across his bottom lip. His great lumbering body shakes off two assailants like they're insects and then he boots it straight through the goals. I run up and slap him on the back then go back to my position.

I grin at Pizza Face, giving him a quick bird as he scowls back. "You'll be grinning on the other side of your face in a minute, bum boy."

214

"Winners are grinners, mate," I laugh and turn away. I feel him grab my shoulder and spin me around. Then he hits me—it feels like a train, a runaway horse, a cannonball. His knee comes up with all his weight behind it and powers into my stomach and chest. My breath bursts out of my mouth, and I fall to the ground, writhing in panic as I try to inhale. The pain in my chest! I have to suck air, but it's agony, as if iron bars are squeezing my lungs. I take tiny sips of air and then see him raise his boot, almost in slow motion, to stomp on my face.

Then he's gone, knocked aside by a roaring, red-faced cyclone. It's Brown! Brown grabs my attacker as he falls and then his knee lifts, not to the boy's stomach or chest but right between his legs with such force that the boy jerks backwards, his body curling in agony, tears gushing down his pimply face. I see Brown surrounded, four boys all trying to get in as many kicks and punches against him as they can, and then I see him go down under three of them as the fourth one lifts his big, hairy leg back and aims it straight at Brown's face. I close my eyes, but nothing can stop me from hearing that horrible crunch as his boot connects.

By the time I open my eyes, the umpires are there, and the boys have scattered, leaving the three of us lying there with the stretcher carriers fussing around us. Brown's nose is bleeding so badly I can't see the bottom half of his face, but as he's lifted onto the stretcher, he opens his eyes, winks at me and grins, a gory grimace of victory. Instead of his sharpened teeth, however, there are just bleeding gums. His teeth are gone. I try to grin back, wincing as I struggle to breathe, and he reaches out and pats me awkwardly on the arm. Then I'm jolted painfully off the ground and into the sick bay.

"Couple of broken ribs, I reckon, laddie," says a familiar voice. I nod weakly—there's not enough air to waste on talking—and then everything goes dark.

*

I awake to the sound of muffled whispers and try to sit up, but the pain in my chest knifes through me, and I fall back, gasping.

"He's awake!" says Archie jubilantly, and the door pushes completely open. He, Aaron, Tim and a couple of other kids tiptoe in with Mr Robinson behind them. I twist my head and see Brown—head thrown back, mouth wide open and nose taped—snoring softly in the bed next to me.

"Looks like the King Brown's had his fangs pulled," says Aaron quietly, "but it took a mob of them to do it!"

"He saved my neck," I answer, talking in gasps. "That kid had already trodden on my hand and kicked me in the ribs, and he was about to stomp on my face except that Brown stopped him."

"Stopped him thinking about girls for a long time too!" sniggers Tim, and they all laugh softly. I try not to. It hurts too much. My hand throbs a bit, and I see that it's bandaged.

"How do you feel?" Mr Robinson asks.

"Not bad. I can breathe now at least. Who... Who won the game?"

"We did!" Mr Robinson's eyes twinkle. "Not exactly the best example of AFL I've ever seen, but you played well. The other coach was pretty embarrassed about it."

"They weren't expecting us to be any good, sir. They wrote us off as losers."

"You played better than them, that's for sure," he nods.

We hear a snuffle from Brown's bed, and he grins, his missing teeth and puffy face making him look like the ugliest baby in existence.

"How's the face feel, Brown?" Mr Robinson says.

"Better than hith ballth, thir," Brown lisps, and

everyone roars with laughter, Mr Robinson's bass as loud as any of us. I can't help but laugh this time even though I'm gasping with the pain of it.

"Keep it down in here, can you?" a gruff voice growls at the door. "Sorry, Robbo, didn't see you there."

"No, I'm sorry, Doc. We'll go now and leave you in peace. Young Brown's the man of the moment." We turn and applaud. Brown reddens, but his gappy smile is wide. "Come on, boys, let's leave the wounded soldiers to get a bit of rest."

They file out, waving at us both as they go. The door closes and the room is silent.

"Thanks, mate," I say.

"No worrieth." And we lean back on our pillows, battered and sore but happy.

CHAPTER TWENTY-ONE

Brown and—to a certain extent—I get a fair bit of attention over the next few days. Brown becomes an object of congratulations and praise instead of one of fear and dislike, and the change in him is total. He even walks differently. The aggressive strut is gone, and despite the gaping hole when he smiles, his face softens. After he comes back from the dental clinic in Perth with new teeth, he even looks pretty good. He is never going to have anyone bashing at his door to make him the next James Bond, but now he looks like a big, hefty bloke with a face like a fairly friendly bulldog. I can't really pinpoint what flicked his switch from aggro-head to okay bloke, but I don't care. I owe him. He hangs around Archie a fair bit now, and me too, when we're in the gym. We still eat at our own tables, but the atmosphere has changed and we joke around like old friends.

*

The routine is pretty much the same every day. The boys in the cottage accept me as a kind of stray dog that wanders in every morning; they're nice enough to me and happy to have me around, but they make it clear I'm not meant to be there.

Maths and Science are pretty straightforward, but English is my weakest subject. I can spend ages working on an assignment and scrape through, or I write something in a hurry that I think is a pile of rubbish and it gets a good mark. There seems no plan to it, unlike the other subjects where everything is straightforward—either wrong or right.

The term ends, and we have a short break from classes, but study goes on. On Friday, Mr P says to me, "Give your normal work a rest for a week or so. I just want you to read and think and write about anything that comes to you. Or not." He grins crookedly. "Here, start with this. The title might give you a laugh." He hands me a battered old red book that is leather-bound with gold inlaid letters, *Crime and Punishment* by Fyodor Dostoevsky.

"Very funny, sir."

"Thought you might like it," Mr P calls over his shoulder as he closes the door.

I have the choice of joining my old class with Mrs

220

Shiels for the break or staying in my cell for the morning and studying. I choose my cell. I've gotten used to working on my own, in silence. I sit at my desk that Monday and open the book to the first page. Someone has written in it in Polish, and though I can't read it, I imagine it might be Mr P's mother.

The thought of Mum slices through me, and I remember sitting on the kitchen table with Mum putting on my shoes for me, her soft hair bent beneath my nose, the faint smell of shampoo and, well, just Mum—fresh and clean with her endless supply of white T-shirts and dark-blue jeans. I shake my head, get rid of those thoughts and start to read.

It starts off in that old-fashioned, wordy way, but within a few pages, I'm hooked. Man, those Russians can write. They have a way of creating another world, a world that pulled me into it so that when I stopped reading, I almost felt disoriented for a while—as though I was still living in the land of the story.

Anyway, this guy Raskolnikov is a young student who owes money and is really poor. He gets it into his head that a greedy old pawnbroker who charges very high interest on the money she lends out to all the students should die. His reasoning is that this crime, wrong as it might be, would be far outweighed by the good her death would do; all those students, including himself, would be freed of their debts and able to continue their studies and do great things, contributing to society rather than feeding off it as she had done. So he kills her and steals her money. It's a bit of a bummer, but her sister turns up at the apartment while he is still there, and he has to kill her too.

The rest of the book revolves around his argument that there are two kinds of people in the world: the ordinary and the extraordinary. Raskolnikov believes the extraordinary ones have a duty to break the law under special circumstances in order to benefit humankind, so what he has done is—to him— completely justified and almost a noble, heroic thing.

I think about this. It's a bit of a jolt to think like that, although I guess if any of those plots to kill Hitler had actually worked, no one would have jumped up and down and screamed, "Murder!" It would have stopped the war, and millions of people, including the Jews, wouldn't have suffered and died. Anyone can see that would have been a good thing.

Was this book saying I had done the right thing in killing Reid? I know he was no Hitler, but how long had he been hurting Katy? How evil a thing was that? What if it hadn't been stopped? Katy might have run away and turned into a druggie or even killed herself. My head is buzzing with these thoughts, but underneath, as hard as I am arguing with myself, there is that familiar black pit inside me—that terrifying knowledge that I killed two human beings. How can I argue that away?

Raskolnikov was having a lot of trouble with it too. He kept fainting and getting sick. His argument might be fine at an intellectual level, but it seems to be having a bad effect on him. He's afraid of being caught but acts in such a weird way that it's obvious everyone suspects him.

We still go to the gym every afternoon, and after we work out, we usually buy something from the shop and sit around and talk. My mind is still buzzing about the book, so I say—pretty hesitantly because our conversations don't usually get too deep and meaningful—"I'm reading this book at the moment."

Aaron, Archie and Neil are leaning back against the wall in the rec, knocking back Coke and chips and looking pretty shagged from the gym. I press on and tell them about it. Funnily, they sit up and listen, so I feel like a teacher at story time. When I finish, there is silence.

"Well, what do you think?"

Aaron speaks first. "No, I don't think he's right. You'd have everyone running around and killing people they saw as stopping them from getting what they want. You could kill your boss who was going to give you the sack and justify it by saying that if you lost your job, your family would suffer, you'd lose your home and car, your kids wouldn't have a good education and so on. Maybe I could rob a bank and kill someone but justify it by saying I'm going to use that money to help people." He frowns and shakes his head. "No, that's a crap idea."

"What about you, Arch? What do you reckon?"

"Aaron's right. I didn't think of it that way, but of course if everyone thinks they're above the law—or what did that writer say? 'extraordinary'?—there'll just be a bloodbath. Like it was before there were any laws." He pauses and looks me straight in the eye. "It's never right to take someone's life. If they attack you, you defend yourself and maybe they get killed. That's another thing. You can't go out and cold-bloodedly knock someone off just because it suits you."

He turns to Neil, who's been listening to us. Neil looks a bit surprised and frowns, taking a few moments to work out his answer. "I don't think anyone should take anyone's life, ever, for any reason. No death penalty. What if you get it wrong? Just the chance of stuffing up and someone getting executed wrongly. Man, what a shocker. That's enough reason to never take someone's life."

There's a pause. Archie speaks quietly, almost to himself. "Big weight to carry around for the rest of your life, though—killing someone. I guess that's the real punishment."

Aaron breaks it in his usual way. "Heavy convo, bros!"

"Yeah, I know," I say defensively. "Got to use our brains sometimes, don't we?"

He nods. "True. We haven't used 'em much so far, have we?"

"Nah," says Neil. "We're all dumb to be in here when we could be out there, having a good time…"

"We'll get there," Archie breaks in, excitedly. "Only three more months, and I'm out. Home, and I'm never coming back."

Aaron opens his mouth to make a flip remark, and then, looking at the determination in Archie's face, he shuts it again. "All this talk's made me tired. I'm going back to my cell till tea." He doesn't look as good as he used to. Something has changed in him. He doesn't hold himself like that golden boy I'd seen running around the oval any more. He keeps his head down, makes no eye contact and kind of slinks away.

Archie and I watch him go. "What's wrong with him?" I ask. "He looks sick."

"He's not sick; he's just hooked on that crap that poxy guard is bringing in for him. He's not tired, either. He just wants a fix," Archie mutters.

"How does he afford it?"

"What makes you think he pays with money?" Neil broke in darkly. "That guard's a pig. He's got Aaron hooked, so he knows he'll do anything to keep getting his stuff. Sometimes being ugly's a bonus. Pretty boys like Aaron get targeted by slime like him." He shrugs. "Maybe there *are* times when someone shouldn't live. Nah, not really, but he needs to be stopped for good somehow."

"You're right," says Archie, "but keep out of it. You won't win taking on a guard. I hate what's happening to Aaron, but I can't afford to get mixed up in it. Three months—that's all I have to last. The best way I can help Aaron is to be a friend when he gets out. He'll always have a home wherever I am—he knows that—but I can't risk getting caught up in this shit. If I have to do any more time, especially in prison, I'm finished."

Neil and I glance at each other, and thankfully the siren rings, and we move off.

CHAPTER TWENTY-TWO

A lot of what happened is a complete blur now. I mean, it's clear to that point where I did what I did, but then I sort of shut down. There were policemen, and I just went along: "In here; sit down there; what happened? Why'd you do it?" They were actually pretty nice to me, I think. Maybe they just thought I was some sort of lunatic.

I remember getting my blood taken, I think, but I was coming down off those drugs; and everything was weird. I felt like I was a zombie, a body without a mind. Just one foot after another, sit where I'm told, tell them my name—did I know what I'd done? Yes, yes, but why? Then everything would stop, and I'd hang in that empty space, somewhere far away. Eventually their voices would fade, and time would stop.

And that's how it was. I remember Mr Bloom—a lawyer who said he was trying to help me—as well as the remand centre, the hard bunk, the face of the guard, the court room, the judge, and what was being said, but I was recording it like a camera would. I was disconnected from everything, even Katy. I saw her on the stand, but she didn't look at me once. She just kept saying, "I don't know why." She wouldn't want to tell them all about him; I understand that. She couldn't be expected to tell them all about Reid and what he did.

Underneath all the horror and self-loathing, there was a tiny grain, a tiny little light deep in that darkness—Katy was safe. I had saved her! It had gone horribly wrong—I hadn't meant it to happen like that—but Katy was safe now.

You know the rest.

CHAPTER TWENTY-THREE

I write down my thoughts on the book for Mr P, plus what the boys had said. I actually like Raskolnikov, the hero, even if he is a bit of a wuss, fainting all over the place—but then I guess we all act differently when we're in a terrible spot. I hand it in to Mr P the first day back, and he raises his eyebrows at the amount I've written. While I work, he reads it over.

"Good comments, Luca—both yours and your friends. Let's make this one of the novels you use for the exams. You've got a good grasp on it already."

I feel relieved. I thought he just gave it to me to read over the holidays as something to do, but I feel pretty good about this book. This Russian guy was like me. He'd killed someone—two people in fact— he had a sister he was trying to look after, he had a good friend (Archie was mine), and he was pretty sure he'd done what he had for a good reason. Only not the second person. Oh, Mum. My poor mother. God. Stop.

I breathe deep. The bit I don't really get is that he's happy at the end even though he's going off to prison in Siberia for eight years. He could have gotten away with it.

But he was in worse pain before; he was suffering, staggering under the knowledge that he had caused two people's deaths and wasn't able to tell anyone about it. He's suffered so much, and all that suffering is illuminating. The Buddhists call it 'enlightenment' when we see the absolute truth of all things.

The next day, Mr P comes in with a couple of books for me. One's a Buddhist book, *Awakening the Buddha Within*, and the other one's the New Testament. "Two perceptions on suffering. The best you'll ever get."

"Trying to convert me, sir?"

"Not exactly; they'll help you to understand the book. But then," he grins at me, "I live in hope."

*

Believe it or not, a whole year has rolled around. Tomorrow is my birthday. Seventeen. Licence. Car. End of high school. School ball. Girls. Going to the beach. Girls. Parties.

I get the usual card from Mr Khan and another unsigned one with another photo. This one has me, Katy and Dad in it. I put it next to the first one on my desk, and then I look back to what I wrote in my journal this time last year.

Some things have changed, but other things have stayed the same. On the outside, I'm still stuck in this little cell, doing the same things every day. Why I'm in here hasn't changed, and the uncertainty of what will happen to me is still hanging over me, more and more strongly the closer I get to 18. On another level, though, I have one really good friend and quite a few others I like who seem to like me, Neil isn't the dangerous snake I was afraid of, I'm fit, I'm learning and working hard, and I have a great teacher.

Time goes by quickly, whereas every day stretched endlessly back then. I don't know whether that's a good thing or a bad thing. I still crave more air, more sky, and the idea of swimming or running along a beach with the sun on my back is a distant dream, just like girls. I try not to think about Karol anymore, but it's difficult—especially late at night when I can't sleep. That skin: smooth, golden, tiny blonde hairs glinting in the sunlight. Not mine. Tim loves saying that he's off to visit Mrs Palm and her five daughters, and it always gets a laugh, but I think we all hate it. Who needs to be reminded of what else they're missing out on?

The pain over what I've done is always there, but even that's changed. Sometimes I don't even think about it for a whole day! It must be a bit like Gary's eye. He probably doesn't think about it, and then he catches sight of himself in a mirror or someone—a girl he's talking to, maybe—stares at it or, just as bad, looks away. Then he remembers it, and he must think for the millionth time, like me, *if only*. He can't kid himself any more than I can. It's what he is now—Gary, the kid with one eye. And I'm Luca, the boy who killed his own mother and stepfather.

Owen wishes me happy birthday, and I find five dollars on my desk later. The unexpectedness of it brings tears to my eyes. The boys slap me on the back and talk about the cars we'll buy one day.

"I want a big Land Rover," Archie says. "Black and shiny and beautiful."

"Like you!" Neil laughs.

"Dunno about the beautiful part, Neil," I say. "You've been in here way too long if Archie's starting to look hot."

"I'll go anywhere I want to," Archie continues. "On

my own sometimes, but there's plenty of room for other people too. Just get up and drive whenever I feel like it."

"I want something loud and proud," Neil says. "A chick magnet. Mag wheels. Great sound system. I'll drive down the road, and everyone will turn and look. What about you, Luca?"

"A motorbike. A big one, like a Harley. Wind in my face, sun on my back, long, straight road in front of me."

We sit in silence for a moment, imagining how good it would be. The only one sitting there saying nothing is Aaron. He just stares into space, his eyes blank. All the life seems to have drained out of him. His skin, once so smooth and golden, is pasty and pimply. His eyes are no longer twinkling and ready for a joke. He often doesn't even answer at the table when we talk to him—just picks at his food and then goes back to his cell.

As we walk out after breakfast, Archie slips me a piece of paper in an envelope that he must have had in his tracksuit pocket. It's a painting, only it's the size of a birthday card. He's got the blue sky, the red earth, a few scrubby bushes dotted here and there, and three white parrots heading towards the haze of purplish hills. It's all tiny but perfect. I put it carefully on my desk, propping it up next to my birthday card, and then it's time for class.

Mr P has bought a cake, a sponge with jam and cream, and it tastes amazing with my Milo that Norbert has made extra-large. But it's back to work pretty quick for all of us. Exams are creeping up.

Funny how life is. Just when you feel almost happy, rising above some of the crap, something comes to chuck you right back down into it.

CHAPTER TWENTY-FOUR

The next Sunday, I walk back towards the rec, past all the guys lined up for visiting day. Owen sees me and beckons me over. "You've got a visitor. Better get in line."

My chest thumps, like a big kick in my chest. "I don't think so." My voice sounds quivery.

"In line, mate." He smiles and moves off. I step behind Johnno, his usually morose face almost happy. "Dad's coming today," he says, looking away from me after he says it, acting real casual. "Mum's here every week, but I haven't seen Dad for six months. They're not together." He stops.

Hell, I've sat at a table opposite this guy for over a year, and that's the most I've ever heard him say.

"Who's here for you?"

My heart clicks its heels a couple of times. "No idea."

He nods, and the line starts to move. I check myself

over quickly. I look okay for a jailbird—my hair's cut, my nails are clean, my clothes are fine. Suddenly, I'm getting shoved through the door as the boys make a beeline for different tables.

Then I see her. She's thinner and her hair is different, but it's her. Katy. She's sitting at a table, her hands clasped tightly together on top of it and her eyes down, but the second I'm through that doorway, she looks straight at me, with an expression on her face like she doesn't know whether to smile or cry or both. I get to the table and reach for her hands, but she pulls them back, and her face is set and grim, just like Mum's used to be. I sit down opposite her, confused.

"Hi, Luca," she says at last. "Happy birthday for last week."

"You too." I grasp for something to say—anything—but she speaks first.

"Dad asked me to come and see you."

I blink. "You've seen Dad?"

She looks at me, frowning a little. "Of course. So have you. He was in the court, sitting at the back."

"I never saw him."

She shrugs. "Well, he was there. I can understand that you don't remember seeing him…"

"Didn't see him," I correct her.

"Didn't see him, then. Whatever. You were acting so weird I can understand that nothing much was registering with you."

"But you've seen him," I repeat.

"Yes, of course. I stayed with him and his wife; he remarried, by the way, after..." Her voice trails off but not for long. "Aunty Alma sold her house and moved into Mum and Ray's house." Her voice shakes a little, and she stops. After regaining control, she goes on. "She looked after me. I don't know what I would have done without her. I finished school last year, and I've been working here and there in Geraldton, doing nothing much, and now she wants to go back east and take me with her. She has family there, and I want to go too. Start over." She looks squarely at me for a long moment. "I don't ever want to come back here. The house will be sold, and that will be an end to it."

"But what about Dad?"

"He has his own life now and a new family. I didn't feel at home there. Don't get me wrong—he was good to me, and his wife couldn't have been kinder, but I wanted to be with my friends and I missed Aunty Alma. She's been like a mother to me... almost." Her mouth thins into that hard, straight line. "Dad keeps in touch. He does his best, but he and I were never as close as you two. It was me and Mum, remember?" She tries to maintain the tough expression, but her eyes fill with tears, and she brushes them away angrily with the back of her hand, just like she used to when she was a little kid.

She takes a deep, shuddering breath, and whispers, "Why did you do it, Luca? What had Ray done to you that was so bad? I get that Mum got in the way—not that it helps much—but what set you off? Or was it just the drugs?"

I look at her, my face twisting into an expression of disbelief. "What had he done to me? Are you serious, or have you blocked it out of your mind?" My raised voice brings one of the guards over.

"Tone it down, or your friend will have to leave."

I nod, and the guard saunters away.

Katy is staring at me, her mouth turning down at the corners in disgust. "What, because he didn't make a big fuss of you like Dad did? Because you weren't Luca, the carrier of the family name, the perfect child who hung on his father's every word?" Her voice was low and venomous. "Was that worth killing him for? And my mother along with him?"

It is my turn to stare at her. She gulps and makes an obviously superhuman attempt at controlling herself.

"Look, Luca, this isn't why I came here. I just came to say…"

"Why the hell do you think I did it?" I hiss.

She looks down, and I can see her jaws working as though she's gritting her teeth. "I know you didn't know what you were doing. You were high on speed." Her voice drones as though she's said those words many times, either to herself or to other people.

"Katy, what do you remember of that night?"

She glances at me and then turns away.

"The house was dark. It was late. Ray was talking to me, and you switched on the light and then went completely berserk." She stops, breathing hard. "That's all I want to remember."

I sat there, listening to the tick of the clock on the wall, the murmurs, the laughter, the urgent talk around me. I have to make her see it. Even if I can't tell anyone else about it, there has to be honesty between us. No lies.

"So Ray was sitting on your bed, half-dressed in the dark, with his arm around you, and you were crying."

She stares at me. "My God, Luca. You don't… you didn't think…" She stops, and her eyes fill with tears. The tears spill down her cheeks, but she still keeps looking straight at me, her gaze never wavering. Her hands unfold, and she takes my hands on the top of the table, gripping them hard.

"Luca, you've got to listen to me." Katy breathes hard and then begins speaking, her voice low and clear. "The day before, we'd gone to Dongara for my game on Sunday. Erin came too. She was my best friend."

I nod impatiently. "I know all that."

"There was someone on the boys' team I really liked—Kim. I'd met him down at the beach a few times, and we'd kissed and all that. We were an item."

"You never told me."

"We were way past the times when we shared everything, Luca. You were so wrapped up in yourself and mourning Dad and hating Mum and Ray."

"I never hated Mum," I say quietly.

She pauses. "It seemed like you hated everyone. Even me."

"Just him. Never you or Mum."

"Just let me tell you! Saturday night had been great. Erin and I had gone with all the kids, both teams, down to the beach. We'd lit a bonfire, cooked sausages, sung songs and danced, and then everyone had kind of quietened down and just sat around the fire. I was lying there, looking into the coals, everyone's voices droning away, and I must have gone to sleep. You know what I'm like."

It was true. She was full of energy, but when her head hit the pillow, she'd be asleep in under a minute. Dad used to call her Quick Snore McGraw when she was little.

"I woke up later, and it was cold. Only a few kids were left on the beach, so I stood up and looked around for Erin and Kim. I couldn't see them, so I figured they'd gone back to the hotel. I was pretty pissed off, as a matter of fact. Mum was going to growl if it was really late, but then she knew exactly where I was, so I figured it couldn't be that late after all.

"I was walking back on the path through the sand hills when I heard Kim's voice. I opened my mouth to call him, but then I heard Erin's voice giggling, so I stopped and stepped off the path towards their voices. The moon was fairly bright, and as I climbed over the hill, I saw Kim and Erin lying under a blanket. Kim was on top of Erin, and Erin's arms were wrapped around him. Neither of them saw me standing there, my shadow almost touching them, and I don't know how long I stood there till I turned and left. Erin came in much later, and I pretended I was asleep. She tiptoed around, and within five minutes, she was asleep.

"The next day, both of them acted just the same, except I saw the looks and smiles they gave each other. I said nothing, but when we dropped Erin off, I walked her to her door and said, 'Don't come near me at school. Don't come near me anywhere'. She looked shocked, and then she ran inside. I said I was tired when we got home and stayed in my room." She gives a twisted little smile. "I was sadder about Erin than Kim; another boyfriend I can always get, but Erin and I had been friends since Day One at high school.

"Ray heard me crying. He didn't want to wake Mum, I guess, so he knocked on my door quietly and came in without turning the light on. I told him everything, and he was so kind, Luca, so kind." Her voice trembles. "Just like he always was. He told me how something similar had happened to him once. He made me feel better. He was about to go back to bed when you switched on the light."

My mind is running in circles. I pull my hands from hers and bury my face in them. I'm shaking—not just my hands but somewhere deep inside, just like I was when I was in court.

Katy's hands are on my shoulders. "Luca, Luca, you made a mistake, a horrible mistake. Ray was helping me; he wasn't abusing me."

My head jerks up. "Why didn't you say something in court?"

"I thought you'd just gone crazy on drugs. I didn't want to say how much you'd always hated him, so I just kept quiet. Like you did. I thought I would make it worse for you if I said anything, and I was so angry at you, Luca. I hated you for what you'd done." She was crying openly now, her face red. "My poor brother, you got it all so wrong."

The guard comes over again to see what's going on.

"Thank you. I'm all right," Katy says, smiling shakily up at him.

"Time's just about up," The guard says quietly, and Katy blows her nose, carefully dabbing under her eyes and wiping away watery, mascara rivulets.

"I see Dad every now and then, but I've got my own life now. So has he. I came down to say goodbye to him before we leave next week, and he asked me to see you. He talks about you all the time, Luca." She shrugs. "Nothing's changed."

The bell tinkles for everyone to say their goodbyes.

"I'm glad I came to see you. Maybe in a while, when you're out of here, we'll see each other again. I don't know. I just want to leave everything behind and start afresh—new job, new home, new people."

I nod. How can I blame her?

"Good luck, Luca." Katy smiles, and the tears slip down her cheeks. "We won't be able to see each other right now, but I'll be just around the corner, just like when we were little." And then she's gone.

I feel a touch on my shoulder and jerk my head up. Everyone has left, and I'm sitting alone at the table.

"Pretty girl," the guard says. "Your girlfriend?"

I shake my head but can't speak.

"Time to go now. I know it's tough when they go and you can't go too, but it won't be forever."

I stumble back to my cell and sit on the edge of my bed, shaking, and then I roll myself into a ball, and despite everything, I sleep.

CHAPTER TWENTY-FIVE

At lunch, I know Archie's talking to me, and I nod when he stops but don't hear what he's saying. After a while, the conversation slides around me, and I feel like I'm in a bubble, cut off, unable to think, eat or speak.

Later, I sit at my desk and open a book, but nothing's going in. I sit there staring blindly till lights out, and then I lie in the darkness, forcing my mind to stay in one place. I go over everything from the time I saw Katy till she left, concentrating on every detail so it's burned into my brain: her hair, her clothes, her hands, her voice…what she'd said. Then I stop thinking and start shaking again, lying there and staring into the darkness till morning comes at last, and it's not till the room is misty and grey that I finally sleep.

*

I sleep in the next morning. I always wake well before the siren, but this morning, I wake groggily, partway through some dream, that sound cutting through everything. I lie there with my eyes still closed, and I know something is wrong. What is it? Then it floods back, and I open my eyes and count the bricks in the end wall, forcing my mind not to think.

It's breakfast, and Archie peers at me, his hair flopping forwards towards those soft eyes. "Feeling better today, mate?"

I nod but can't look him in the eye. My mood is contagious, and the boys sitting at the table all turn quiet, eyes lowered. I sit there, trying to look preoccupied and thoughtful rather than just totally on another planet. I just can't shake this zombie feeling. I know the only way I can keep things together is to push every thought down deep, away from where I have to consciously look at it and realise what I've done, realise what I've… I concentrate on my food, chew every bit carefully, carry my plates over, go back to my cell and get ready for class.

I walk across the quad by myself now, without Owen. There are always a couple of guards on duty anyway in case someone has a go at climbing up the fence or onto the roof. I knock on the door, still in zombie mode. I can do this. I've done it before, and I can do it again.

The door opens, and it's Mr P. He's early today. His mouth is moving, but I can't really hear him. Then my knees buckle, and I'm on the ground, rolled up in a ball, sobbing! God, is that noise coming from me? He's lifting me up and half-carrying me inside, but I can't stop; I can't stop!

I'm in Norbert's room, curled up on his bed and trying to make myself small. My thoughts start to slow. They'll think I'm a lunatic. What am I saying? I *am* one. Outside, in the main room, I become aware of Mr P murmuring something to each boy. The door closes, and a chair scrapes close to the bed. I hear it creak as Mr P settles into it. A large hand closes on my shoulder, stroking it as if it were a cat, but it feels good—soothing—my breathing slows, and my body stops its horrible jumping and tingling. The room is silent. What now?

"What's going on, Luca?"

How can I get out of this? What can I say? I turn and sit up, leaning back on the wall. "Don't you have to teach the boys, sir?" I say, stalling for time.

"They're fine; don't worry about them. They have plenty to go on with. Now, what's happened?"

I hang my head. The silence is pressing down on me. The room seems small, and I finally look up to tell him some crap about feeling sick or something, but when I see those deep-set blue eyes boring into me, I know it's going to be impossible to lie to him. It just starts pouring out of my mouth, all of it. 'Pouring' is the only word to describe it. It's a flood, like some dam inside me has broken and everything is coming out.

Strangely, it seems to make sense, even though I have no real idea what I'm going to say before it's out of my mouth. I tell him about Dad, Reid—how I loathed him—Mum and Katy... everything comes out. He sits there listening, totally concentrating on me and not interrupting. I pause, breathing hard, after I tell him about that night in Katy's room. I can't meet his eyes, and he speaks for the first time.

"Go on."

Finally, I slow down and haltingly tell him about Katy's visit and what she told me. I start shaking again. "It was all a mistake. I thought that as wrong as it was that I had killed him, at least I had protected Katy from him forever—but it turns out she didn't need any protection. She loved him, and he probably loved her. He'd never shown her anything but kindness, and for that he died. I killed him. I can't justify it even in the slightest way. The only thing that's kept me going all this time is that I'd done it for Katy, but now I know the truth. I did it for myself. All that hatred I had built up for so long, and then I saw an excuse to attack him. I hadn't meant to kill him—just to hurt him, just to make him go away.

"As if that would happen," I add bitterly. "Why should he go away? He had my mother, my sister, their house and their life together. I was the problem, not him. Because of my anger, he died; Mum died; Katy lost him, her mother, everything; Mrs Brockman lost her brother. All gone because of me. That's the truth of it. There's no noble heroic deed done by a protective brother. There's just an angry, hate-filled, drugged-up piece of shit that doesn't deserve to be alive. No one should cause that much damage and be able to live."

I stop at last, feeling somehow cleaner than I'd felt for a long while. The truth is out in the open. All that dark poison inside me is gone, spewed up in that outpouring. I know what I am.

The silence is deeper this time after my voice had filled the room for so long. Mr P's head is down. Clearly, he can't look at me because his disgust must be so great. He shifts in his chair, gropes in his pocket and pulls out a neatly folded handkerchief. He opens it slowly, wipes his eyes and then blows his nose.

There is a quiet knock from outside, and Norbert comes in, carrying two mugs of Milo. He puts them both down on the little bedside table and then turns to go. Mr P stands up.

"Thank you, Norbert," he says and turns to me. "I'll just check how everyone is going, and then I'll be back." He goes, and I sit there, the sweet smell of the drink filling the little room. I relish the feeling of peace that comes over me. The worst is out. I'm like a piece of driftwood that's lying washed up on some beach, nothing hidden, nothing left—just the shape of something that once was picked bare.

Mr P comes back in, head down, still not looking me in the eye. Suddenly, he grabs my hands together in his big paws.

"This is a terrible thing you've been carrying, Luca, but it was a mistake—an awful, tragic mistake, but still a mistake." I wait for him to go on, but he says nothing more.

"This isn't just a mistake, sir. A mistake is what you do in Maths, and then you go back, cross it out, correct it and on you go. No real harm done." My voice strengthens. I'm sure of myself now, surer than

I've ever been. "There's no crossing out this one. Two people are dead, and they won't be coming back. It was bad enough knowing that I'd killed someone when I had that tiny bit of excuse to hang on to—that I thought he was hurting Katy. It was still terrible, but now there is nothing—just the cold, hard fact that I've taken lives, one of them my own mother's life, and for nothing. Nothing at all."

Even though I know what I am saying is disturbing, probably as bad as you can get, I am calm. My heart isn't pounding, and I'm not shaking; I'm ice.

"That's true. Nothing can change the result of what happened, but there were things beyond your control that led to it."

"That I was off my face on drugs. Nobody's fault but mine. I took them, no one else."

"They're a part of it, but really, it may have happened even if you hadn't taken anything."

I think about this for a moment. "I don't know. I was totally out of control, and whether that was down to drugs or not, I don't know. It's a blur. I didn't think I was killing him—just hurting him so he knew what it was like."

"So you didn't think a softball bat would kill him?"

"No," I say wonderingly, "but then only a lunatic

would hit someone as hard as they could with a bat and not know it was causing serious damage."

"So it stands to reason that drugs were playing a part in how you responded that night. On the one hand, you say you had no intention of killing him, and yet you picked up and used a bat, which—as you said—only a lunatic would imagine wouldn't do terrible damage."

"Fair enough. But they're both dead. It was partly due to the effect of the drugs, but you still can't change that fact."

"Can anything change that fact?"

"Of course not. It happened, and nothing can change it now."

He smiles at me for the first time. "And will all your thinking about it, all your regret, all your guilt, change that fact?"

I sit silent though I can hear the boys murmuring and kookaburras laughing in the tree in the courtyard. "No," I say at last, "nothing will ever change that fact."

"Then, Luca, you have two choices. You can either remain locked up inside yourself, thinking only of that event, going over and over it even though you know that all the thinking in the world won't make any difference, or..." He stops, locking me to him with those dark blue eyes of his, "...or you can move forward. That doesn't mean dismissing what happened, but it happened; it's in the past. Concentrate now—not on what you did but on what you can become."

The siren rings, jerking me back to the moment. The whole morning has gone! "Sorry, sir," I gasp.

He smiles. "You're worth it, Luca. Now, take it easy today. Tomorrow, I'll help you to grab the steering wheel of that mind of yours." He opens the door, and the boys look up from their packing up.

"Well done, boys. Any questions?"

"Nothing that can't wait till tomorrow," Norbert answers, and the others nod.

"See you, kid. Keep your pecker up!" they chorus as I try to sneak out.

I smile at them, embarrassed, thinking yet again how different they are from the other boys in this place. They're keen to get on with life and make a new start. Quite a few of the boys in the main building are pretty much dead-heads. You can just tell by looking in their eyes. Life's kicked them in the teeth too many times, and they've given up and turned nasty or vacant. I guess I just tried to become numb.

CHAPTER TWENTY-SIX

I go to lunch and see the boys already sitting down. Archie glances up as I come over, and I see a small frown crease between his eyes.

"Hi, Arch, guys. Sorry I've been such a boring pain in the arse. What's been happening?"

Archie's face splits in a grin, the crease disappearing.

"Nothing much, man, but it's a pretty special day today."

"Why?"

They look at me and laugh. "You must have been out of it, dude," says Tim. "He's been talking about it every day since last week."

"Exactly one month," says Archie, quietly, and though those big white teeth of his are neoning in my face, I see the tears in his eyes.

"That's amazing, Arch!" I reach over and slap him on the back, but even though my grin is almost as

254

wide as his, my chest tightens. What am I going to do without him? As though he knows what I'm thinking, his smile fades.

"Yes, it is, but the bad part is that I won't see any of you mob. I won't even be able to visit because I'm heading straight back to Carnarvon."

Aaron sticks his head forward from where he's sitting slumped at the far end of the table. "Don't think about coming back in here, Arch, even to visit. Once you're out, stay out. Forget this place and mixing with any losers like us."

"We're not all losers," Johnno breaks in. "There's no way I'm coming back in here." He's more animated than I've ever seen him. "My Dad's got me a pre-apprenticeship set up for when I get out. Just because I acted like a loser once doesn't make me one forever."

"Good luck to you, then," Aaron mumbles and sags back, his head down.

We munch away for a while, and then Tim says, "I'm out six months after you, Arch." We all look at him, surprised. He reddens a bit then, and keen to take the attention off himself, asks, "What about everyone else?"

It's something we've never talked about. Seems to make it harder somehow.

255

"Three months," says Johnno. We go around the table till it comes to me.

"No idea," I say as casually as I can. "When they're ready."

Only Archie knows why I'm in here, but it dawns on the others that I've done something pretty damned serious. There's an awkward silence.

"Neil will be here," Archie breaks in.

"For how long?"

"Another three months here, and then maybe he transfers to prison."

Another silence, more sombre this time. "What did he do?" Tim says—not the way he had said it to me so long ago but quietly, sadly.

Aaron sits forward again and looks at Archie, who looks down at the table and picks at the edge of his place mat, and then he whispers huskily, "He grabbed a girl walking along the street one night, and he and his mates took her and raped her. The thing is he kept her locked up for three days before she got away."

I feel my guts clench in disgust, but at the same time, I think, *Who am I to judge him? At least she lived.* I push the thoughts away.

"You probably heard about it. It was on the news, but they didn't say much about what happened to her—just that she was home safe. The thing is his age would have meant he got off fairly lightly from the rape charge—the other guys were older—but the kidnapping, he did alone, and that's a really serious charge." Archie sighed. "So God knows how long he's got to go."

"Deserves it," Aaron spits out. "Imagine if that girl had been your sister or friend."

Tim blurts out quickly, "This is meant to be a happy day! One month for Archie! What are you going to do first, Arch? Go to the movies? Hungry Jacks?"

"No way," Archie laughs. "I'm staying outside as much as I can. I just want to look up and see the sky above me and no buildings around me. Breathe clean air. Give my mum a hug. Sit and have some good tucker with my relations." He stops and grins wryly. "Make sure none of the kids in my mob end up here. Frighten the crap out of them. Tell them whatever I have to in order to help 'em learn good stuff to do instead of having 'em do rotten, stupid things because they're bored."

We nod, and then lunch finishes. I have plenty of study to do, but I can't concentrate, so I just relax and go over what Mr P said. But what the heck did he mean about grabbing the steering wheel of my mind?

*

It doesn't take long to find out. The next morning, when I go to the cottage, there are pillows and cushions on the floor in a circle, and the chairs are pushed back out of the way. Mr P is already there, and he smiles at me when I come in and stand, puzzled, with my books.

"Ah, you're here, Luca. Now we can start. Everyone kick off your shoes and sit on a cushion. Make sure you're comfortable." There are groans and moans as the boys flop down on the floor. "No, don't lie on the floor, you slobs; like this." Mr P sinks down onto his cushion, back straight and legs folded underneath him.

"It looks weird! I can't do that!" protests Norbert.

"Give it a try. You sat like that when you were a baby!"

We all frown at one another, and Mr P laughs. "Come on, or would you rather get back to your work?"

Everyone scrambles into position. It looks strange but feels okay. As long as your bum is up higher than your feet, you tip forward a bit and your legs balance you when they're folded. Mr P's knees are flat on the floor, but most of ours stick up at different angles.

"Don't worry about what you look like. Just get comfortable. Your legs will flatten down in a while when the muscles stretch a bit."

The guys start laughing and saying "Om", trying to

look saintly, and Mr P just waits. When it quiets down, he says, "Close your eyes. I want you to concentrate on the other senses." His voice is soft and low. "First, touch. Concentrate on your feet, your ankles, the contact with the floor—and let them relax," and so he goes slowly, from our toes to the tops of our heads. Then it's taste, the inside of the mouth, the tongue lying soft. Then sound—no thinking about it, just experiencing it. It's pretty restful, really, slowing down everything like that.

Finally, he gets us just to concentrate on our breathing, counting each breath slowly to 10 and then starting again. The thing is to follow your breath and not start thinking about anything else. Man, that's hard! It sounds so easy, but just try it! I get to four or something and then I'm thinking about what maths I need to do today or about Archie leaving—anything but counting my breaths.

Mr P must know what's happening because he says, "Don't worry when your mind wanders. This takes practice. Just become aware you are following your thoughts, let them go and start counting again."

After a while, he tells us to open our eyes. My God! Half an hour has gone by! It felt like it has only been 10 minutes. Everyone looks a bit stunned.

"How was that, boys?"

We go around in turn, and everyone says pretty much the same thing—how hard it was to stop thinking! "I'll never be able to do that," Norbert says, shaking his head. We all nod.

"You probably said the same thing the first time you got on a bike or started learning to read. You'll get better the more you practise. Now we'd better start some work."

We go to our desks. Everyone is very mellow, and it's much quieter than usual. Ten minutes before the siren goes, Mr P asks us to pack away. We look up at him, surprised—he usually goes to the wire—but we do as he asks.

"How did your work go today?" Mr P asks.

"I got heaps done," I say. "More in one hit than I usually do." The others murmur agreement.

"Why do you think that is?"

"Well," says good old Norbert, "it was like we'd had a chill pill before we started, so I guess even though none of us seemed able to quiet down our thoughts to count to 10, they were still quieter than usual, so we could just concentrate on what was in front of us." That sounds about right to me, and I see others nodding.

"That's after one 30-minute session, boys. Try it for the rest of the day. When you're eating lunch, concentrate just on your food—the flavours, the textures, the smell—instead of wolfing it down and thinking about something else. If someone speaks to you, give them your whole attention rather than thinking about your response or about something else."

The siren rings but no one moves. Mr P raises his eyebrows.

"Sir," I say, knowing I speak for the others, "can we start the day off the same way tomorrow? We easily made up the time."

"Of course," he smiles, "but remember, you can do this anytime. You can always practise being present— your mind in the 'here' and 'now' and not in regretful thoughts of the past or even hopeful thoughts of the future. Just here. Now."

Walking out the door, something hits me. Mr P really practises what he preaches; it's why I talked to him so easily yesterday, why I feel so good around him. He just listens so well. It seems like he's drinking in every word, not thinking about anything else like I guess most of us do. I know I get distracted pretty easily, at least. It's such a corny thing to say about a person—"He's really there for me"—but with Mr P, he really is. There is nowhere else for him. I smile to myself. So that's what he meant by taking the steering wheel of my mind!

Lunch is just ham sandwiches and some fruit, but I take my time and let the bread soften on my tongue, the saltiness of the ham starting my mouth watering. I finish one mouthful completely before taking another. The others are prattling away, food hanging out of their mouths as usual, but I resist the urge to join in and keep chewing away, relishing every bit of flavour. Finishing a banana and reaching automatically for another one, I realise I'm full—my mouth isn't on auto pilot—and I sit back, content. Tim is talking to me under his breath—he can be such an idiot—but I fight down that thought and try listening to him.

"Luca, I'm really worried about Aaron."

"Where is he?" I ask, turning to look, surprised I hadn't noticed him missing.

"He's over in the infirmary. He collapsed in class this morning. I reckon they know he's on drugs but can't work out where they're coming from. Johnno heard him telling Archie that the way to make the time go fast in here is to be high all the time and it's worth doing anything to get his hands on the stuff."

Chapter Twenty-Six

"I think that guard..." I start, but Tim breaks in.

"Johnno saw the guard coming out of Aaron's cell when he was on the laundry shift. He snuck off real fast. Guards aren't meant to be in there with the doors closed. Who else could it be?"

I remember the day of the footy game and the way the guard had hovered around Aaron, touching his shoulder—too close to him, way too close.

"You're probably right. How about I say something to Mr Khan? If they do a blood test on Aaron, they'll know he's on something, and if I tell them where it's coming from, they'll stop him."

Tim looks at me, a mixture of disbelief and panic in his eyes. "Man, you can't do that! They'll know it was you!"

"So what? Surely they'll get rid of the guard, and that'll be that."

He shakes his head emphatically. "You just don't get it, do you? That guard will be supplying plenty of guys in here. They won't be happy if their supply dries up. But that's not the main thing; you'll be a dog, a rat."

"What do you mean?" I burst out louder than I had meant to, and several heads swing my way. "The guard's the one doing something wrong, not me!"

"Doesn't matter. You never dob anyone in, even if it's a dirty pig like him."

"But he'll be gone," I persist, "and Aaron will be safe!"

"Maybe. But you'll get bashed, and the guards will all hate you. You never dob, no matter what."

"Okay, I get the bit about the drugs drying up if he goes, but what's it to the other guards?"

"He's one of them, and that's that. He'll lose his job, and it'll be down to you. It's not Fairyland in here, Luca. There are rules you don't break, and the main one is you don't ever be a dog. No one will speak to you—no one. Even Archie."

"Even you?"

"Even me," he nods without hesitation.

Perplexed, I shake my head. "Well, I'll be out of here within the year. I'll be in prison."

Tim shakes his head. "You don't reckon guards know other guards, crims know other crims? There's no network like the one in prisons. Then you'll really be in the shit. You'll get stuck in a cell with some filthy, violent pig, you'll get all the worst jobs, and the other guys will either keep away from you or give you a hard time. No one wants a dog for a friend in prison. They might be thought of as a dog too, so something gets said that shouldn't be said, and they get blamed along with you. Birds of a feather and all that."

He's silent at last, and lunch finishes. "Just remember, if you think a juvenile detention centre is tough, you'll feel like you're going to die in prison. Don't make it a certainty. Keep your mouth shut."

I'm the last to leave the table, and Archie raises his eyebrows at me as he pushes in his chair. "Lost in thought, Einstein?"

"Just thinking about Aaron."

"It's a good thing he's in sick bay. They might get him off that crap now if only that scungy guard will keep away from him."

CHAPTER TWENTY-SEVEN

The next morning, I cross to the cottage as soon as I've cleaned up and knock on the door. It's so quiet! I can usually hear the boys mucking around, clearing up their breakfast things and laughing and joking. The door swings open. It's Jason. He smiles at me in his shy way and motions me inside. The boys are on the cushions, eyes closed, legs crossed. I pull off my shoes, grab a cushion, sit down as quietly as I can and wait till my breath calms down, and then I start counting to 10 like Mr P showed us yesterday.

We hear the front door click, but nobody moves. We hear Mr P's shoes on the floor, and then he sits down and everything is silent once more. My breathing is slow, and my mind is soft, just floating on each breath. I have never felt so calm.

After a while, Mr P begins speaking. "Just let your closed eyes rest on a point somewhere in front of the bridge of your nose. Keep breathing slowly and let you mind be still now. No need to count. Just observe your mind. If a thought pops up, let it pass gently. Don't follow it. Just watch it go as if you were standing in a high window, watching a passing parade. A thought might intrude into your mind, but just let it pass. Keep breathing and watching for the breaks between thoughts."

This is harder than counting, but it is so good to have that night start to replay in my mind as it's done thousands of times and to just let it go—just watch it dissolve while I'm sitting calmly, breathing quietly. It's gone.

"Okay, boys. Open your eyes." We sit there, smiling. Once again, we talk about what it was like. Some boys say nothing. I'm one of them.

"Don't just keep this for here. If you wake early, sit on the floor on your pillow. Even five or ten minutes, if you can."

As we start getting up from the floor, Norbert says, "Sir, it's good to sit quietly, but what is really the point of it?" We stand still, and Mr P waves us to our seats.

"Good question. Can you keep it till tomorrow? There's one more step to this that might help answer that question."

We start work quietly. We've all got a fair bit to do now—revision, checking notes, going over old exam papers. Not all the boys are doing exams, but the year is coming to an end, and they have modules of work to finish for their courses.

*

That afternoon, in the gym, Owen comes over to Archie and me and says, "You've got permission to see your friend." We put down the weights and follow him down the corridor. We sit on the bench outside the sick bay door while Owen goes in.

"He must be pretty right if they're letting us see him," Archie says. He looks happy, but his right leg is twitching fast, up and down, up and down.

Owen sticks his head out of the door. "In you come."

Archie goes through first, and I hang back. I glance around, remembering the room well from the time after the football game. Now, there's a boy of about 13 in one of the beds, his head thrown back, mouth wide open, snoring softly. There are some posters on the wall about not smoking, not taking drugs and treating people with respect. Captive audience, I suppose. Another boy, one I know, lies back in his bed, reading a car magazine. He looks up and smiles at me, putting the magazine down.

"Hi, Ben," I say. "What're you in here for?"

"Nothing much," he says, his hand brushing unconsciously across his forehead, where there is a blue-green bruise. "Just slipped in the shower and hit my head." I nod. We all know about that one. He's pissed somebody off for sure. "Kinda' nice in here, though."

I wander slowly to where Aaron is sitting on his bed, knees crossed, pyjama top undone, gazing listlessly at Archie.

"You'll be out of here soon after me. Just hang on till then."

Aaron shakes his head. "Listen, Arch, I don't want to get out of here. What makes you think it's so great out there?" He stops and frowns. "Why didn't they just leave me alone? They had no right to pump my stomach. It's my life and my decision to end it. None of their business, interfering arseholes."

Archie gets up from the chair beside the bed. "I'm not listening to this crap," he says and strides off to the door. Neither of us say anything for a minute, and then Aaron shrugs and says, "You know what I mean, don't you?"

I panic for a second. What's the right thing to say?

Don't rush. Think. I breathe slowly, and then it comes to me.

"No, I don't, Aaron. I've taken the lives of two people—one I loved—and the thought of another person I think a lot of dying as well is just more than I can take." My voice breaks, and I close my eyes for a moment. Breathe. Just breathe. I feel a grip on my arm. I open my eyes, and Aaron's staring intently at me, his brow furrowed. There's no vagueness in his look now.

"That's heavy."

"Don't try it again, Aaron. Archie's right. You'll get past all of this."

"There's no one out there for me, Luca. My mother has her own life. She never wanted me in the first place. I don't even know who my old man is. Some loser, I guess. The only thing that's ever made me feel good is drugs. Oh yeah," he grins, "and sport." His smile fades, and his eyes go dead again. "I can't do without drugs, and I can't do… I can't do what I have been doing to get them. Not anymore. I'd rather be dead." He grips my arm again. "You get that, don't you?"

I nod. "I get it, but listen; I meant what I said. I can't take another person around me dying. I haven't got anyone out there either. No one. Will you just hang around for a while? For me?"

He smiles sadly. "I'll die without drugs anyway."

"I'll get them for you!" I hiss. "I've only spent a bit of the money in my account. I'll get the word out, and you'll have what you need."

"But there's still the guard. Nothing will stop him from coming into my cell."

"I think I've got a way to stop him."

Alarmed, Aaron sits up. "Don't say anything, Luca, or you're dead meat."

"I know all about that. I can do it without telling them anything they don't already know. Promise me you won't do anything stupid till I speak to you again."

He smiles. "I can't promise you I won't do anything stupid, but I can promise you I won't neck myself just yet." Just for that moment, the old Aaron is back.

Minutes later, I'm outside, where Archie is waiting for me. He's sitting on the bench with his head in his hands. "Luca," he says. "I'm gonna have to stop that guard. I was trying to keep clean till I got out, but what sort of friend am I if I don't help Aaron? He's going to be dead if I don't do something." He laughs hollowly. "Not much point being out there free if I've left a mate to die." He gets heavily to his feet.

"Archie, don't do a thing. I have a way."

He stops and turns. "What way?"

"Just don't do anything yet, okay?"

Archie nods, puzzled.

Owen wanders across. "How's the patient?"

"Not bad. Do you think I could see Mr Khan?"

"Sure. Let's see if he's busy."

We start back up the corridor, but Archie pulls me back. "Don't do it. Don't say nothing."

"I won't, Arch," I say and lope off next to Owen.

Five minutes later, I'm sitting opposite Mr Khan.

"What can I do for you, Luca?" he smiles. "Nothing wrong, I hope?"

"Nothing that you can't help fix, sir," I say confidently, although I'm feeling a bit shaky inside. He waits, and I take a deep breath. "My friend Aaron is in sick bay. I guess he'll be out in a day or two, and I want to stop him from hurting himself again."

He raises his eyebrows, leaning forward slightly in his chair. "Are you going to tell me where he got the drugs from?"

"Sorry; I can't help you with that."

"Then what can you do?" Mr Khan frowns.

"I'd like Aaron to move to my cell, sir. A double bunk can go in there, and then I'd be able to keep an eye on him, keep him off the drugs."

Pursing his lips a little, Mr Khan says, "You could

272

be sure of it if you found out where he was getting the drugs from." I say nothing. "Most boys prefer their own cells. It's very unusual to give up a single cell."

I have to convince him. "I know that, sir, but he's been a good friend to me, and if someone's there with him all the time, he won't get the opportunity to do anything."

Mr Khan sits there for a moment, rolling the pen on his desk back and forth. "Well, if you're sure about this, I can move you both to a shared cell and someone else can have your single ones." I feel a pang. My cell has been my cocoon—where I've written to you in my journal so often—the only place I could be myself. "That'll be great, sir."

He smiles at me. "Not for too long, though. Your new cellmate gets out soon."

*

I pack up my few things, and Owen takes me to my new home. It's a bit bigger than a single cell, but I know once Aaron's in here, it'll be pretty squeezy. I set up my desk—my journal on the bottom so Aaron doesn't see it—and my clothes, and I take the top bunk. Later that night, while I'm studying, Aaron wanders in, his arms full of his stuff.

"What's the deal, dude?"

I wait till the guard leaves and closes the door. "No one's going to be coming in here without my knowing it. You're never going to be alone in here. He's not going to do a thing while there's a witness."

Aaron purses his mouth. "I feel like a little kid, though, with you watching me all the time."

"Don't you think you need it?"

He frowns for a second and then slowly nods. "Guess this is my bunk."

"Yep. All you have to do is shut up when I study."

"No big deal." He potters around, sticking posters up over the walls and stacking his clothes away while I finish, and then we both hit the sack. We talk for a while and then say goodnight. I'm just drifting off when Aaron says, "Luca?"

"What?"

"Thanks."

"No worries."

CHAPTER TWENTY-EIGHT

The day before Archie leaves, we have a bit of a party. The boys on kitchen duty even make him a packet cake and cut it into the shape of a key like they do for people's 21st birthdays. Archie's face is just glowing. That's the only way to describe it.

"I'll see you soon, anyway," he says, and then he frowns and glances at me.

I shrug a little. "We know, Arch."

Next morning at breakfast, everyone whistles and cheers when Archie comes in wearing a checked shirt and jeans, his hair wet and brushed back but with some of his curls pinging back down his neck and above his ears already. He waves like the champion he is, and Tim even gets his breakfast tray for him. We laugh and joke, but breakfast is over too soon, and he'll be gone by lunch time. The boys troop past him, and just Aaron and I hang back. I step up to Archie and hug him.

"Couldn't have lasted without you, mate," I say. He doesn't answer, but I feel his body tremble, and I walk away quickly. No time to brood though; it's straight over to class for the last time. What a day of goodbyes.

We're pretty good with our meditating now. If ever there's a good drug, meditation must be it. We're all hooked. I don't just sit there counting now. I start that way to slow my thoughts down, and then I just let my thoughts pass. After a while, everything's calm. Mr P says to stay with whatever feeling comes up—even if it's a bad feeling, like being agitated; just acknowledge it and feel agitated. Don't think about what's making you that way—just stay with the feeling till it passes.

Most often the feeling that comes up in me is sadness. When I used to think about what I did, about Mum and Ray, I'd feel so many thoughts all clattering and banging into each other—guilt, self-loathing, fear, horror, disgust—but now all that's left is sadness, a sadness that I think will be with me forever, but I accept it. Today, though, my mind is full of Archie, and I feel happy, so happy for him. I sit and feel that happiness, and I can't help but smile.

There's only a little group of us doing our exams. The other boys are lying around on the couches or in their rooms, but they join us to wish Mr P a good holiday and to thank him for all he's done for us.

Jason stands up, grinning with embarrassment. "We'd just like to thank you, Mr P, for working with us all this time. We've bought you something to remember us by." He hands Mr P a parcel. I have no idea what it is. I'm not included. All I've done is written him a letter thanking him for all he's done for me. I step forward and put the letter on top of the parcel.

Mr P stands there, a big smile on his face. He scratches the back of his neck and hitches up those awful pants he wears. "Thank you, boys. It's been a privilege and a pleasure."

"Open your present, sir," urges Norbert. The other boys laugh.

"Okay, okay." Mr P rips open the package, and out fall a pair of jeans and a T-shirt.

"Time to get a bit groovy, sir. Hope they fit."

"He won't notice if they don't!" We all laugh, including Mr P, because we all know it's true.

"Well, I've got a little something for each of you; nothing much—nothing as flash as your present to me." He hands us each a parcel, and I can tell mine's a book. Bet it's another Buddhist one! I rip the paper open and look at the back. Yep. On the back cover, it says something about someone called Milarepa, who lived over a thousand years ago. He'd caused the deaths of 35 people, but he changed his life around through meditation and became one of the great heroes of Tibetan Buddhism, achieving enlightenment in one lifetime. Typical Mr P. The allusion's not lost on me. See? I've learnt what an allusion is this year!

Mr P comes over. "Good luck, Luca. I'm proud of what you've done this year. It's been a pleasure to know you." He turns to the boys. "How about we just spend the last few minutes on our cushions, boys? Just something a bit different to finish off."

Surprised, we sit down again. Whatever Mr P wants to do, that's fine. His funny clothes, his raucous laughter, his mellow, soothing voice—they'll all be gone for good in a little while, so we settle, smiling at him.

"Just close your eyes. I want you to imagine somewhere a long way off, a beautiful valley. There are snow-capped mountains around you, and the valley is green and lush. Slowly, it fills with countless Buddhas, sitting like you." He pauses. "Or, if you prefer, it can be Jesus standing there, smiling down on you. A soft, white light comes from them, joining together in a glowing purity all the way down to you. It surrounds you and then flows gently through the top of your head and into your body, filling it with light and love. Any dark parts in your body—where you hold fear or pain—dissolve in that radiant light until your whole body is filled and surrounded. You are pure. All pain is gone. You are healed."

He stops talking, but I hardly notice. Those dark parts sure are in me—I can feel it in my stomach and chest when I think about that night—but that light fills me, and even though I know it won't last, that feeling is good. I wish I could just sit there forever.

"Well, boys, that's it." We open our eyes and blink at each other. "Stay where you are," Mr P says, getting to his feet. "I'd like to remember you all this way."

Jason says in a husky voice, "You wouldn't have one dark place in you. You're good all the way through."

A tiny flinch contorts Mr P's face for a second. "We all have our dark places, Jason. Knowing that helps us to have compassion for everyone else." He waves gently to us and is gone.

We sit in silence for a while, and then I say goodbye to them all and thank them for having me, just as did the first time I came. They laugh, and I leave with a smile on my face.

I see Neil that afternoon in the gym.

"Can you get some speed or whatever it is that Aaron takes?" I ask.

Neil screws up his face. "You going to turn into a crack-head too?"

"No, no. I just need to have some for when Aaron needs it."

"Sure. I'll sort it. Go to the shop on Tuesday or Friday and tell Brett—the one who does the book, no one else—how much you need. He'll transfer the money from your account. He'll just give a total to the guy who supplies at the end of the day, and he'll take stuff to that value. Neat, huh?"

"Will he give it to me straight away?"

"Hell no, but you'll get it soon enough." A couple of guards come into the gym, and we get back to our weights.

I follow Neil's instructions, and the next day, when I'm on duty in the kitchen, Stephen—a skinny little kid I know only by sight—leans on the bench next to me. He talks like we're great mates, and as he turns to go, he slaps me lightly on the chest. I finish wiping down the bench and then step back to check out what happened, scratching my chest near my pocket. Yep, two bumps at the bottom of it. I'm nervous, but I carry on as normal, working and chatting till my duty is over and I'm back in our cell. Aaron's in the rec with Neil. We've agreed that he isn't to be here on his own.

I glue a couple of pages of notes together around the edges, leaving the top open, and then I drop the pills in. I slide the pages into the middle of the rest of my notes and then paper clip them all together. Aaron comes in a few minutes later, and I feel his agitation. Neil must have said something. Bugger. He should have kept his mouth closed.

"Hi," I say, turning back to my book.

"Luca," he says. I look and see him fidgeting with the edge of his blanket.

"What's up?"

"I know you got some stuff for me."

"I said I would." I hand him the pills, and he looks at them lying in his curled palm like fat white slugs. He licks the corner of his mouth, not taking his eyes off the pills as though they'll disappear if he looks away for an instant. Finally, he raises his eyes to meet mine.

"Here," he says, handing me one back. "Keep this for another time." I take it wordlessly and go back to my books. I hear the creak of Aaron's bunk, and once his breathing slows down, I slide the other pill back in its spot. I don't know what this stuff is, and I don't want to know, but I won't judge him for taking it.

CHAPTER TWENTY-NINE

After all the long build-up, the exams are over in a matter of days. I think I did okay, except I could have written so much more in the English exam. I've lived with Raskolnikov for months, and I think I'm able to understand and identify with him, but I don't really write that fast.

Now I just have to wait. I've applied for the same degree course in Maths and Science at four different universities, although I don't really know what I want to do and part of me doesn't even want to think about it. I feel a bit lost now with no study. I miss the cottage; I miss Mr P; I miss Archie.

Mr Robinson peps up the sport a bit, and we play cricket every weekend. It's not really for me, but just being outside is worth all the slowness of the game. Geez, I'd shovel horse manure all day if I could be outside in the sunshine. Mr Khan asks us all to organise a concert for Christmas. Some of the guys sneer at first, but some guitars and drum kits get dragged out from somewhere, and there are auditions. It starts to be fun. We have some singers, a band and a play that's pretty stupid, but gradually, more boys start hanging around and the guards get involved too.

I read a lot now—the Buddhist books and the Bible. I can't believe they are really saying the same thing: love one another; have compassion for one another. Same message. The Buddhists spell it out pretty clearly. They have these four basic ideas: the Four Noble Truths. Basically, they're saying life is difficult. They got that right. The reason it's like that is that we crave satisfaction. It's true. We're always wanting something other than what we've got.

I was once so desperate for a bike that I thought if only I had one, I'd be happy forever. Within a few months of getting it, however, it was getting rusty because I dropped it on the ground instead of putting it carefully away, and it started looking old. Then Gary got a brand new racing bike. Mine looked so crappy next to his, and all I could think about was getting one like his and comparing my bike to his. We lurch along all the time like that—always wanting something bigger, better, newer.

The third thing that leads on from this is that there's a way out of this endless trap for everyone. Just stop all this craving for things, this constant greed. I'll have to think about that one. Even if I'd somehow got Karol as my girlfriend, would I have gotten sick of her down the track? Found fault with her and wanted a prettier or smarter girl or whatever? People always seem so happy on their wedding day—as though they've got everything they want—but just look at how many get divorced.

The final step is a big one. It says there is a way out of all this: living a life of virtue, wisdom and meditation. Well, I haven't got much of the first two with the way I've stuffed up my life, but I love meditation. Mr P says the word comes from the same base as the word 'medicine'—they are both connected to healing, and some part of me feels like I'm healing.

Back to the Buddhists. Once again, they break it down for you—a real road map to follow. They call it the Eightfold Path. Basically, you don't look outside yourself for someone to wave a magic wand and make life happy; instead, you look to yourself. Jesus says the same thing: the Kingdom of Heaven is within you and available to everyone.

Anyway, I'll shut up now before I bore the crap out

of you. Just read some of those books and learn how to meditate. Think before you act. Unless, of course, you've already got it all together. But I doubt it.

I don't know how to tell you. I've sat down half a dozen times to write, but I just can't believe it, and I end up staring at the wall in amazement while my mind goes over everything again. Here goes.

Mr Khan called me in a few days ago and said that Dad wanted to see me but first wanted to make sure that I was willing to see him! I sat there, stunned. I let happiness wash through me, but there was something niggling at me. Of course. It would be like when Katy came. She can't forgive me for what I've done, and Dad will be the same. He loved Mum so much... but I have to see him. I'm prepared for everything he has to say; he won't be saying anything I haven't said to myself a thousand times.

I nod speechlessly to Mr Khan. He smiles and says, "Good. He's waiting in the visitors' room for you. You'll have it to yourself."

"Now?" I gasp. "He's here now?"

"Yes. He's been with me most of the morning." Mr Khan stands up.

"Thank you," I say stupidly and leave. I don't remember how I get down the corridor; my heart is hammering so hard, and then I'm through the door, and it's Dad—oh Jesus, Dad—and his arms are around me, and we're both laughing and crying like a pair of fools.

He steps back at last, and we look at one another. He hasn't changed a bit, except that there are a few flecks of grey in his hair and he's put on a bit of weight. I drink him in, every feature: his dark eyes, crinkled at the corners; those little white lines where he squinted into the sun and those bits haven't tanned; his big, bony nose; everything. At last we sit down.

"You've grown so much, Luca! You're nearly a man."

"I work out a bit, Dad." It feels strange but so good to be saying that word again. There's so much to talk about, but we fall silent. That heavy sense of sadness weighs me down, and I sink into a chair. Dad grips my wrists.

"I didn't think you'd see me, Luca."

"I thought you'd forgotten all about me," I whisper huskily.

"Never! Never! You've never been out of my thoughts." His voice catches, and he stops for a moment. "Can you ever forgive me?"

"What for? You and Mum broke up. You left. It happens all the time."

"What for? I abandoned you. I thought I was doing the right thing by getting out of the way. I was just thinking of myself! I saw that when…it happened. I just couldn't stand seeing you every now and then, being a part-time father. I couldn't separate you and your sister, and she couldn't leave her mother. I drove back past the house one afternoon, and Katy was with him, holding his hand and skipping along beside him, and they were both laughing away. I just assumed you felt the same way."

"No, Dad! I hated him!"

Silence.

"I know that now. I didn't know then. I didn't even think of it." Dad shakes his head. "What a terrible thing I did to you, Luca. Look at what my stupidity caused." He covers his eyes.

"No, Dad. It wasn't you. I did it."

Dad shakes his head sadly. "Katy told me what really happened. You were doing what I'd always taught you to do: trying to look after your family. Great one I was to say it. I didn't look after you at all." He lets out a long, shuddery sigh. "Can you ever forgive me, Luca?"

He's been suffering just as much as me. He blames himself for all of it. I grip his arm, feeling the strong, sinewy muscles I know so well. "Of course, Dad; of course."

His body sags for a moment, and then he sits up straight. "I've seen your lawyer and told him all that Katy told me. He took a statement from her before she left."

"What do you mean? What does it matter what I said to Katy?"

His eyes light up. "Don't you see, Luca? This changes everything."

"Nothing's changed. I killed them…both."

He sighs. "But you never explained what happened that night. It seemed like a random, vicious, drug-fuelled attack, but it wasn't. You were provoked. You thought Reid was abusing Katy, and you—a 15-year-old—ran at him in your anger, and he punched you. What you did next was self-defence."

"But I was on drugs, Dad!"

"Certainly that was a factor. The thing is, Luca, almost anyone would have acted the same way."

"But I was wrong, Dad," I hung my head, "so horribly wrong and… Mum… That shouldn't have happened." The tears are running freely down my face now, but I don't care.

Dad nods slowly. "No one acts rationally when

they're filled with wrath, with rage. Your mum was just in the wrong place at the wrong time."

We sit there for a long time. I hear the noise in the dining room as the boys get ready for tea. I just want to keep sitting here.

"The thing is, Luca, Mr Bloom is sure you can leave here and come home with me into my care. I've spoken to Mr Khan, and he only has good things to say about you. But it's not just up to him. There'll be a hearing…"

"Court again?" I break in.

"No, nothing like that. They'll hold it here. Maybe they'll keep you here till you're 18—I don't know—but then, Luca, then," his eyes twinkle at me again, "you'll come home."

A thrill runs through me, but at the same time, I think, *Where's home?* Katy had said that Dad was remarried now, but just the thought of leaving here takes my breath away for a moment. I haven't allowed myself to think about it as something that would actually ever happen, but just for this little time, I do.

"You'd need to speak to a counsellor or a psychologist, Mr Khan said, but there's a good chance, Luca; there's hope. Who knows, you could be out by the time you turn 18."

Two warring feelings are battling away inside me.

I could be out in just a few months! But then that word I hate: hope. That's just fantasising, imagining something's going to be different from what you've got right now. I will myself to calm down, and I begin to breathe slowly for a few seconds till I hear the door open behind me.

"Time's up," the guard says, and Dad and I stand.

"Whatever happens, Dad, thanks for coming."

Dad bows his head. "I'll be back on Sunday. I won't desert you a second time, son." He reaches across and grips my hand, and we stand there for a moment, like two people just being introduced, and then I turn and go.

CHAPTER THIRTY

Later that night, I'm lying on my bed in that weird half-awake, half-asleep state when Aaron whispers, "You awake?"

I jerk fully awake. "Am now. What's up?"

"Sorry. Do you think I could have the other one?"

"I'll get it in a sec. Can I talk to you first, before you're off the planet?"

There's a silence for a few heart beats, and I'm just about to say, "Don't worry about it; here's your stuff," when Aaron says, "Sure."

Then out it comes. I tell him about what happened today and how good it was to see Dad. He interrupts me every now and then to ask me things like why Dad hasn't been to see me before and who Katy is so that, before I know it, he gets the whole story.

When I finish, he's quiet for a bit then says, "Do you think you'd have done it if you weren't high?"

"I'll never really know. I think maybe I'd still have tried to hurt him in some way, but the thing is I would have been aware of what I was doing; I would have seen Mum, or realised that it was her, and I would have also realised the damage I was causing. The way I was, I was just in some strange vacuum where I knew I was doing things, but I was disconnected from them. It was like they weren't real. I might have heard what Katy was saying or maybe that first belt in the face might have stopped me, but I was in a bubble, and I think that was probably the drugs." I stop. "That's why I hate drugs so much. They take your brain away. They make you like some sort of animal, really—functioning and feeling but with no control. Mr P once said to me that there is a steering wheel to your mind and you've got to be the one with your hands on the wheel, not the drugs."

"Being on drugs is like driving with no hands on the wheel," Aaron says. We lie there for a while, and then I swing my legs out of bed and go over to my desk, picking up my notes where the pill is hidden.

"Don't worry," he says. "I'll be okay."

"You sure?"

"Not really, but I have to try sometimes. Trouble is I have tried before so many times, but I can't keep it up." He laughs drily. "I'm a weak prick, Luca. I'd really like to get off it, but it seems to be the best thing in my life at the moment, and that's pretty hard to give up. But, hey, that's such good news about your Dad and everything."

We don't say anything more, and in a few minutes, I hear his breathing become even. How's he going to make it on the outside? I roll over to go to sleep, frowning a little at the thought, but the day has been too good for me to stay worried about anything tonight, and I go to sleep with a smile on my face.

*

Aaron's looking better. He's started taking an interest in sport again, and though I'm still getting him drugs, he's cut right back. I praise him for trying so hard but say nothing when he asks me to get him more. That's why I feel so shocked when I go into our cell one afternoon and all my books and notes are on the floor. Someone's trashed all my stuff, and the pages where I hide the drugs are ripped open. Shit. It can only be Aaron. I've never actually hidden where I'm keeping them from him, but he always asks me to give them to him. It's some sort of manners he has, I suppose, because I buy them for him. I sit there, feeling really pissed off. Even the spines of the books Mr P gave me have been cut open to make sure there's nothing been stuffed down there.

I hear someone stop outside in the corridor. The door's still open, and turning, I see Owen. I smile at him, but he averts his eyes.

"Mr Khan wants to see you." He says and steps back, waiting for me to come out and stand in front of him, something he stopped doing ages ago. We usually walk together now, but today it's back to how it was when I first came in here.

Mr Khan looks just as severe. What the hell? He motions for me to sit down.

"You've disappointed me, Luca. I'm not very often so wrong in judging the boys in my care, but you've certainly fooled me." He sees the puzzled look on my face and continues. "Too late for the innocent look. Drugs have been found hidden in your cell." He folds his arms and leans back in his chair, waiting for me to speak, but what can I say? The moment stretches on agonizingly, and finally, he breaks it. "I remember you sitting right there, Luca, and telling me you'll never take drugs again." Still I say nothing. To speak is to betray Aaron.

"Well, I'm not the only one disappointed. Your father will be also. He has been in constant contact with me—as has your lawyer, Mr Bloom, who has been working on your behalf—and you do this." Mr Khan is silent again, and when I still say nothing, he adds, "I was very impressed with your desire to help your friend, Aaron, but now I can see that you were only thinking of yourself. No doubt he is able to get drugs for you and that was behind your request to get him in with you."

My throat is dry, but I manage to croak, "I don't take drugs. Blood test me, Mr Khan. You'll see I'm telling the truth."

"If that's true, the only reason you're hiding them in your cell among your things is that you're dealing." He shoots a disgusted look at me. "So handy to have one of your customers in the bunk above you. No wonder you wouldn't tell me who was supplying your friend with the drugs even though you clearly knew."

I can't meet his eyes. I must look like such a liar, staring at that gold leaf pattern on the desk with my jaw clamped and nothing to say.

Mr Khan stands and opens the door, where Owen is waiting. As I leave, he says, "Things were looking very promising for you, Luca. All destroyed by this stupidity."

As we walk silently back to the cell, that pig of a guard who started all this comes over and speaks to Owen. As he walks off, he grins at me—an evil, self-satisfied grin—and I know that it wasn't Aaron who went through my stuff at all. The guard must have figured out Aaron was getting it somehow and taken the gamble that it was stashed somewhere in the cell. Well, he was right, and he won.

I sit at my desk, too shattered to do anything about the mess, when Aaron bowls in. "Shit, what's gone on in here?"

I tell him, my voice dull and lifeless. He's apologizing to me—I can hear him—and I'm murmuring that it's not his fault, but I don't want to talk. Closing my eyes, I turn away and lay my head down on the top of my wrecked books.

A few minutes later, the siren goes for duties. I get slowly to my feet. Aaron's already left, so I pad down to the library and start going through the books that lie waiting to be marked off and returned to the shelves. It's mechanical, mindless work—all I feel capable of, even though I usually like it, flicking through the books and putting aside anything that looks good. For the first time, I really feel the urge to drug myself out, wiping out my thoughts—especially the look I can imagine on Dad's face when he finds out about this. Looks like Ray Reid was right. I may as well be zonked out under a bridge.

It's because I let myself hope. How stupid. Haven't I learned anything?

Aaron isn't at tea that night. I hear the others ask about him, and I tell them I don't know anything, but I can guess he's figured out there'll be no more stuff from me now with our cell under constant surveillance, so he's gone off looking for some other source—the well's dried up as far as I'm concerned. Maybe he even wants the drugs so badly that he'll go and talk to that guard. Winners are grinners. Whatever made me think I could do some good for someone? I'm just a dirty little killer; no point pretending anything else.

I'm in my cell later that night when Owen comes in. He doesn't say anything, but the hard look's off his face. "Just getting your mate's clothes," he says, and he opens the cupboard and drawers and bundles up Aaron's few things. "He says you can have the posters." Then he's gone. Aaron must have asked for a new cell. Yep, he's done a deal with that guard for sure. Everything I tried to do has come to nothing.

I start cleaning up my books. A torn page flutters to the floor from one of the Buddhist books Mr P gave me. There is a quote on it from some Buddhist saint, *All the happiness there is in this world comes from thinking about others, and all the suffering comes from preoccupation with yourself.* I can't keep the sneer off my face as I screw the scrap of paper up and throw it in the bin. That worked out really well for me; I did all I could to help Aaron, and look where it got me.

Life isn't worth living. What's the point? The thought keeps echoing in my head as I sit there, and I know that there's only going to be one way out of this for me.

CHAPTER THIRTY-ONE

I wake up in the middle of the night. How can I do this? I need to do it well and finally, not stuff it up like Aaron did. This is no 'cry for help'; I want out, permanently. I feel so totally alone—even the tossing and turning from Aaron in the bunk below me is gone for good. I know that Dad won't give up on me now, no matter what, but what's the point? I'll just bring him trouble. He has a new wife, a new life. I lie there trying to think clearly, and then I feel my ears tickling. You sad piece of shit, Luca. Your tears are running down the sides of your face and into your ears. I stop myself laughing. I can't afford to let any emotion out; who knows what might happen? Some crazy outburst like with Mr P that day?

I'm dreaming. Katy and I are playing chasey in the back yard. She's laughing and running away, and even though I know I'm faster, just when I put my hands out to grab her, she's gone! I hear a noise, and she's behind me, still laughing. I turn and try again. Each time, she disappears. Finally, I grab her shoulders, but an awful noise is coming from her. Stop, Katy! My eyes fly open, and it's the siren blaring. I blink a few times, disoriented for a moment, and then everything comes back to me. I close my eyes again, and then the door opens.

"Up you get, Sunshine. Mr Khan wants you." It's Owen, but he looks quite chirpy. Just an act, obviously; it's all an act. He waits outside while I wash and dress quickly, and then when I go to fall in behind him, he strolls along beside me.

Mr Khan is having a coffee and toast when I come in. "Thank you, Owen."

What the hell is going on? I haven't even had any breakfast, and my stomach growls.

Mr Khan laughs. "I won't keep you long. Here, have a piece of toast."

I'm so shocked I take it and look at him uncomprehendingly. He nods, and I wolf it down while he munches his toast and drinks his coffee deliberately and slowly. He says nothing while he eats. One thing at a time, I guess—no talking to people with a full mouth and all that.

Finally, he turns to me. "Interesting day yesterday, Luca. Very satisfying day." I gulp. Yeah, great. Who for? He wipes his mouth and hands carefully, opening his top drawer and checking his face in a small mirror. He presses a buzzer, and a guard comes in and takes his tray.

"I had a visit from your young friend Aaron yesterday. He told me the whole story."

I feel myself go cold. "How do you mean 'everything', sir?"

Mr Khan leans forward on his desk and looks into my eyes, a thin little smile playing on his lips. "I mean everything: where he got the drugs in the first place and how you have helped him get out of that situation. He said that apart from Archie, you're the only true friend he's ever had and he couldn't stand by and see something bad happen to you when all you were trying to do was to help him." He pauses, leaning back and folding his arms, and then continues. "He said knowing you has made him want to be a better person and not just a selfish druggie. He didn't think he had much chance getting off drugs, but he said that knowing what happened in your life and your struggling with it but still caring about people and trying to do the best you could made him think he just might give it a shot. He knows you hated giving the drugs to him after what they did to your life. He wants to repay you for what you've done for him."

I sit there, dazed. Tim's words about not being a dog sound in my head. "But sir, his life will be hell in here now. He'll be branded a dog."

Mr Khan's thick, dark eyebrows raise, and he tilts his head a little. "That's why I wanted to speak to you so early, Luca. Aaron isn't even here. I took a statement from him about the guard in question and organized immediate placement for him in a drug rehabilitation halfway house. His time in here was almost up, and he's in the custody of the people who run the house. He'll have to stay there beyond his original sentence, but he's more than happy to do that. He says it's his only hope."

"Where?" I ask stupidly. This is all going a bit fast for me.

"In the country. He's gone into a program that will wean him off drugs and get him back on track. The rest is up to him. By the way, he left this for you." Mr Khan opens the drawer, takes out an envelope and hands it to me across the desk. I raise my eyes questioningly, and he nods, so I take the folded bit of paper from inside and read Aaron's hurried scrawl.

Thanks, bro. There's so much more I want to say to you,

but let's leave it till I've been clean for a year, and then we'll get together with Arch. Don't worry about me. I feel hopeful for the first time in ages. Maybe I can actually do this! At least I've seen what a self-centred knob I've been, and I've figured out that I'll never be happy just thinking of myself and what I want all the time. I want to look out for other people too, Luca—just like you've done for me. I've started with you, and I feel great. Aaron

I fold it back up slowly and carefully, my mind a blank. Mr Khan is sitting back in his chair, his fingertips together, smiling at me.

"What about...the guard, sir?" I ask.

"We've had our eye on him for a while, Luca. Too late now for Aaron, but he'll be taken care of." The smile's gone from his face now, and I see another Mr Khan. Those warm, brown eyes are cold and hard, but then he looks at me and smiles again.

"So, back to you. I have already called your father and brought him up to date. He's a very happy man today, Luca. As for you, I can't condone someone supplying drugs, but in light of all the circumstances, I think the panel will be understanding. If you are still unwilling to speak to a professional, however, that will, shall we say, throw a major spanner in the works." He fixes me with those eyes again, his face serious.

"I'll do anything I have to, sir."

Mr Khan nods. "Good decision. Now go and have a proper breakfast. The situation with Aaron—what's happened, where he is and so on—is strictly confidential. You know nothing."

"Yes, sir; of course."

"Good," Mr Khan says, dismissively. "An excellent outcome. I'll arrange your counselling sessions, and we'll take it from there."

Five minutes later, I'm enjoying every mouthful of my soggy Cornflakes. The boys say surprisingly little about Aaron. They just assume his sentence was done and he left. I guess it's because he's been a ghost at the table for such a long time that he's easy for them to forget. Not for me.

I hurry back to my cell after breakfast and rush straight over to my bin. Thank God it's still there. The little scrap of paper I had tossed away so contemptuously was the same message that had been in Aaron's note. He'd never read it, but he'd learned it anyway. I knew he was smart—smarter than I was. I pull my pillow off my bed and sit, legs crossed and eyes closed, feeling that familiar peace settle on me. Life can be good.

CHAPTER THIRTY-TWO

Things move much faster than I could have imagined after that. First, my results arrive. Mr P has forwarded them on, and he puts in a note congratulating me. I've done okay. In fact, I get an offer from three of the four places I applied to. I talk it over with Dad, and he thinks it might be a good idea to defer till second semester. I might be out by then! We both agree I need a bit of time to get used to things outside. The thought of going straight into a university with a whole lot of people disturbs me a bit. I hate to admit it, but this place has been like a cocoon for me.

There's plenty I can't wait to get out for—the beach, going for a run, just being able to do what I want when I want—but crowds, I think, will worry me for a while. I also don't think this whole process will move as fast as Dad thinks it will. I'll believe it's actually happening when I'm in the car, down the road and out of the gates.

I see the counsellor three times a week. She's very easy to talk to—doesn't appear to judge—and hell, it's just so nice to spend time with a woman, even if she is about 50. She's gentle and plump and smells good, but apart from that, she helps me find ways to handle my black thoughts. To tell you the truth, we end up talking about meditation a fair bit of the time. A lot of the things she says are pretty obvious, but she also talks a lot about handling my grief, something I almost didn't think I had the right to do because I was the cause of it all.

Halfway through January, the Board will hear my case. Mr Bloom says he's quite confident. That 'quite' makes my belly churn a bit, but as I said, I'm trying really hard not to believe this is all going to actually happen. Mr P is going to be there, and Mr Robinson and even Owen have made statements about me, but then the police who came to the house and saw what I had done will probably do the same.

On the day of the hearing, they call me in, and it seems pretty casual compared to being in court. There are people there I don't know, and they ask me questions. I answer everything as simply as I can, but then one question comes at me that I have to think about for a minute before I answer. The person who asks it is tall and thin with sandy hair and thin lips. His freckles remind me of Reid, and I feel the old, familiar sadness.

"How do you know you won't lose your temper in the future, Luca?" he asks, his pale eyes glancing quickly up at me from his notes. "Two people died. Regardless of the circumstances that have been made available to us, that fact remains. How can we be sure that isn't the way you will always resolve situations you're not happy about?"

I feel this is 'make it or break it' time, but that's not the important thing. What's the truthful answer to that question? I take a deep breath.

"Well, sir, that's the thing you've got to be sure about before you let me leave here. I know that. All I can say is I'm not the same person I was over two years ago. I know the cost of what I've done. I've lost my mother forever—my fault—but my sister has also lost her mother, and Dad lost the mother of his children. Everyone who loved Mum lost her, and even though I had no love for Ray Reid, my sister and mother did, not to mention all his family and friends. All those people are paying for what I did. It won't end for them any more than it will ever really end for me. I'll carry what I did to my grave." I stop and rub my hand quickly over my eyes. Shit, they'll think I'm some loser doing my best to put on a performance. *Breathe. Breathe.* I count five breaths slowly, and then I'm in control again. "I know I'll never hurt anyone again. I can't do it. I just know that, but having said it, I trust Mr Khan and my counsellor, Mrs Petersen. If either of them thinks there's a chance I could do something like that again, then don't let me out. Ever. That's all I can say."

There's not the slightest sound when I stop speaking. I can't look at anyone, and then Mr Khan clears his throat. "Thank you, Luca. You can go back to your duties now."

I look at Dad, but his head is bowed, so I just close the door behind me and head for the kitchen. Tim's on duty with me. "Feeling okay, man?" he says, looking at me anxiously.

"Just got to wait now, Tim."

He pats my shoulder and turns back to the dishes he is stacking back in the racks, and I start wiping down the benches.

Mr Bloom has told me that it may be a while before the Board makes a decision, but three days later, Owen comes to the gym and tells me Mr Khan wants to see me. My whole body seems to thud. I shower and dress quickly, and then I go down that corridor knowing my life is going to change one way or another in the next few minutes. I knock on Mr Khan's door, and he calls me in.

Mr Khan's on the phone, so he motions for me to sit down. This is torture, but I quiet myself down as much as I can and prepare for the worst. He hangs up at last and then looks up at me.

"Good news, Luca. The very best. The decision was unanimous, but there are a few strings, of course. You'll need to report to a case manager every week at first, and then, at his discretion and depending on your progress, you will report less often. You'll need to see Mrs Petersen for the first few months as well to help you readjust into normal life, but apart from that, you will be released into the custody of your father."

"When, sir?" I whisper.

"He'll be here straight after breakfast in the morning." Mr Khan stops. I sag onto the table as though all those imaginary cables I was keeping myself in tight with have snapped. I hear the sound of water being poured, and I sit up groggily. Mr Khan is holding out a glass of water, and I take it gratefully. My hand is shaking as I bring it up to my mouth, but I drain the glass. He takes it from me and smiles. "A good day, Luca."

"The best, sir."

I tell everyone at the table what's happened, and they jump up—though it's not strictly allowed while we're eating—and thump me on the back and shoulders. Man, I start coughing with it all, and they think that's hilarious. Even the guards come over and have a laugh. "I'll miss you all," I say when I get my breath back.

"Yeah, right," they all chime in, but they know I mean it.

"You'll all be out soon, anyway."

Tim looks around and nods. "Yep." He sits quietly, staring into space, while the others sit down and get back into the food.

"What's wrong, Tim?"

He jerks and shakes his head, smiling a bit sadly. "Hope poor old Neil isn't doing it too hard in prison." It's not a good thought.

"Hopefully he won't be in there too long."

Tim shrugs. "Funny how he was such a scumbag before, and then he turned into an okay guy. But, hey, this night is yours. Well done, mate."

I look at him closely. Where's the skinny little rat-faced kid gone? He's filled out a bit, for sure, but it's more than that. He's changed. This place changes everyone—some for the better and some not—but he's a pretty good bloke now.

*

I pack up my stuff. There's not much of it apart from my books. I've fixed all the spines as best as I can. I wander down to the rec for the last time, but I don't stay. Behind all the happy words, I see the pain in too many eyes. They want to be going out tomorrow morning too.

I go back to my cell and write to Mr Robinson, Owen and Mr Khan, thanking them all. Then I sit for a while and listen to the noises I've grown so used to over the years here: doors banging, boys laughing, arguing and swearing at each other, the deeper voices of the guards sorting them out, music, televisions.

I feel suddenly tired, and I change and climb into my bunk. I intend to read, but I drift off, calm but a little worried about the future now that I seem to have one.

EPILOGUE

I wake early, in the grey half-light. It's my last morning. I let myself drift, like a seagull on a wind current— half dreaming, half sleeping—till I wake up properly and get ready. I sit on the end of my bunk. I'm too twitchy to meditate, but then I laugh to myself. This is exactly the time I need it, so I spend my last morning in here sitting on my pillow on the floor. It takes me a while to settle, but then I reach that calm place, and though I can feel the excitement underneath it, I'm in control. The siren sounds, but I stay where I am for a minute or two more just to strengthen that control, and then I get up and put my stuff near the door.

The boys are laughing about a movie they saw last night, but they flick quick glances at me and smile. Tim takes my plate and scrapes it clean with his, and then with a final wave, they're all gone. I go back and get my things. Owen comes to my door, and we walk together to the visitors' room. He shakes my hand and wishes me good luck as I push through and see Dad talking to Mr Khan.

"On your way at last, Luca," Mr Khan smiles.

We all stand there awkwardly, exchanging pleasantries, and then Mr Khan escorts us outside. Dad and I step out into the sunshine and cross the gravel car park to Dad's car. My heart is pounding, and I throw my bag in the back and climb in.

"Seat belt, Luca," Dad smiles. God, I feel like I'm six years old. Then we're off, and though Dad takes it fairly slow, there seems to be so much traffic whizzing close and so many people and shops that I feel overwhelmed by it all. Dad's chattering away, but hardly anything registers. My eyes and ears are working overtime, and then I notice he's stopped talking.

"You okay, Dad?"

"Couldn't be better, son. I was just thinking how strange this all must be for you. I thought there might be something you would like to do." We turn abruptly off the highway, the traffic thins and we pass some huge pine trees and go over a hill. There it is, stretching out as far as I can see: the sea. We pull in, and Dad reaches for a couple of plastic bags in the back seat. He throws one at me, and I catch it awkwardly.

"Hope they fit," Dad says. I tip the bag up, and out slides a pair of blue and yellow board shorts. "Feel like a swim?"

Suddenly, I don't care about all the people and cars or anything at all, and grinning at Dad, I open the door and head for the change rooms. Within five minutes, I'm on the beach, springing painfully across the hot sand, and then I'm in the water, under the waves, and I'm laughing and choking on salt water. Dad hurtles past me and hits the water with a roar. We dive under the waves, and I think back—so long ago!—to that day I spent body surfing with Karol. Another life. Another world. But the sea, the sea's always the same. I reckon when I get to be 90, if I can still dive into the sea, I'll feel just the same as when I was 10.

We swim for ages and then go up the street and buy a hamburger, and man, is that good! After we get dressed again, Dad drives around and points out where his parents live. "When you feel like it, the entire family wants to come over and see you. It's been a long time."

Then we just drive. We wind the windows all the way down, and I feel what dogs must be feeling when they hang their heads out of cars.

At last, Dad says, "Well, Uma will be wondering

where we are. She's been planning this meal for your first night home for days." As we head for home, the sun is dipping below the horizon, and I drink in all those colours. God, I've missed the world.

*

We drive towards Fremantle, down the highway, onto the bridge near the old church and across the river. We drive by the harbour, clogged with ships, and then wind through the streets past the little old houses, and finally we pull into a driveway. The house is quite small, with a veranda out the front where four cane chairs cluster near a round table and ferns and palms nestle in the space between there and the little picket fence.

As we stop the car, a woman, carrying a little girl of about two or three, rises from one of the chairs. The woman is delicate-looking, Thai or Indonesian, and she is wrapped in a soft sarong, its colours like jewels against her skin. She smiles shyly as we walk towards her.

"Here he is at last, Uma," Dad says. "Meet my son, Luca. Luca, my wife."

Uma presses her hands together in front of her heart, the way Mr P used to do at the end of a meditation session, and bows slightly. "My son too, now. Welcome." She smiles at me—her smile is infectious—and then Dad laughs.

"We've forgotten the boss of the house. This is Pearl, your little sister." I smile at the little girl, but she buries her face in her mother's shoulder. "She's always shy for a while, but in a few days…" Dad opens the wire door, and exotic smells waft up the passage.

"You must be hungry," Uma says in her soft voice, and I follow her, Dad behind me with my bag. The little girl raises her head over her mother's shoulder and her huge eyes, dark and fluid, lock onto mine. Her gaze is so intense and unwavering that I stop. Can she see straight through me? Does she see what I've done?

Then her arms reach to me, and her mother stops. Those little arms are around my neck, and I lift her into my arms and bury my head into her soft hair. She looks like she would smell of honey and cinnamon, but she smells just like Katy used to when she snuggled up to me.

I'm going to be all right.

www.ingramcontent.com/pod-product-compliance
Lightning Source LLC
Chambersburg PA
CBHW051138030726
47504CB00004B/934